Sometimes It Causes Me to Tremble

Also by Charles Turner

The Celebrant (a novel)
Woman in Light (a play)
The Turtle and the Moon (for children)
The Feast: Reflections on the Bread of Life (with Gregory Post)

Sometimes It Causes Me to Tremble

Charles Turner

LION
PUBLISHING

Lion Books is an imprint of ChariotVICTOR Publishing,
a division of Cook Communications, Colorado Springs, Colorado 80918
Cook Communications, Paris, Ontario
Kingsway Communications, Eastbourne, England

Library of Congress Cataloging-in-Publication Data
Turner, Charles, 1930-
    Sometimes it causes me to tremble/Charles Turner.
    p. cm.
    ISBN 0-74593-867-1
    I. Title.
PS3570.U667S65 1998
813'.54—dc21   97-47783
                                                CIP

Editor: Barbara Williams
Design: Bill Gray
Cover Illustration: Bill Gray

All Scripture is from the *Holy Bible: New International Version®*.
Copyright © 1973, 1978, 1984 by International Bible Society. Used by
permission of Zondervan Publishing House. All rights reserved.

1 2 3 4 5 6 7 8 9 10 Printing/Year 02 01 00 99 98

For my wife

Jo Ann Kachadurian Turner

Every farthing of the cost . . . shall be paid.

Lullaby
W.H. Auden

Author's Note

This is my second novel about a clergyman. In the first, *The Celebrant*, a young Anglican priest followed Christ into the hell that was Memphis in the plague year of 1878. In the present case, a Presbyterian pastor in the Memphis of today finds himself fleshing out in fearful ministry the Word that he preaches.

It is my belief that any serious novel with a Christian theme should deepen the mystery of God and not attempt to shallow it. Although *The Celebrant* and *Sometimes It Causes Me To Tremble* have much in common in that regard, there is one difference that I must make clear: the former was based on historical fact; the novel at hand is a work of the imagination, in which all characters are entirely fictitious.

I am indebted to Rosemary Landon for her ready assistance on project after project and to Larry Potter for his valued counsel.

CHAPTER 1

It was Saturday night and George McKenna was still preparing his Sunday morning sermon. It had been that kind of week. Two funerals. One wedding. His own tenth wedding anniversary. On top of everything else, he felt dry. The sermon he was working on just wasn't coming together. It was panic time.

He cleared the computer screen of a beginning and sat there, his hands poised above the keyboard, waiting. Margaret, fresh from her bath, came in and massaged the back of his neck. The warmth of the tub lingered about her. He smelled the stuff he had given her at Christmas. Slowly, with circling fingertips, the treatment changed. She leaned closer and slipped a hand inside the front of his jersey.

"That's not helping," he said, without reprimand.

Margaret said, "Why don't you dip into the file and pull out a sermon from two or three years ago? Do you honestly think anyone would remember?"

She didn't mean it the way it sounded. George was sure of that. He let the question hang in the air, and she went on and left him alone.

Through the window he could see the steeple, lighted from below, rising above the treetops like some genteel rocket piercing the January dark. He had been pastor of Memorial Presbyterian Church for seven years. This view from his study in the manse never lost its effect on him. It always pumped him up, and then it always brought him down. It filled him with a sense of pride, and then it pricked him with a kind of despair. Memorial was one of the largest churches in East Memphis. The white white of its soaring columns and the very proper red of its brick spoke quietly but unmistakably of the affluence of the membership. The boxwoods lining the circle drive were a fitting accessory to the Jags and the BMWs that prevailed in the Sunday morning parade. What preacher in his middle thirties would not consider this pastorate a prize? But what preacher, if he was serious about his calling, would not be staggered by the responsibility?

His job was to feed the flock and invite others into the fold. It was not as simple as it sounded. He had about decided it was impossible to feed those who did not know they were hungry. As for the business of the rich entering the kingdom of heaven, Jesus had said flat out that it was easier for a camel to pass through the eye of a needle. Sometimes the thought was challenging. Sometimes it was merely depressing.

Tonight, as he sat there wrestling with what to propound in the morning, that statement of Jesus' struck him for the first time as the basis for a sermon. A sermon to be preached head-on, by George McKenna, tomorrow, boldly, without apology. For a minute, he gave the idea the same intensity he might have given the catching of a fish. But the topic was so pertinent it deserved more than slapdash development. He must give it time and prayer.

So his dilemma remained unchanged. The steeple of Memorial Presbyterian Church was piercing the midnight sky—no, it was already after midnight, it was already the Lord's Day—and George McKenna was up against the morning without a sermon ready to go. For the first time ever, he envied those guys who could preach without a sermon written out, even without a developed theme, who simply trusted the Spirit to fill their mouths as they went. He had always thought them highly presumptuous. Besides, he could not bear the thought of everything falling apart along the way and his arriving at the benediction without having made a valid point—or a valid three points, as the fashion dictated. He could not imagine attempting a sermon without thorough preparation and words on paper. Not unless it was something really simple.

Something as simple as, maybe, the Parable about the Good Samaritan.

That was his ticket, it suddenly occurred to him. He leaned back and stretched and thanked the Spirit for bailing him out. Yes, the Good Samaritan. He could wing that one.

Remembering the musty air of Sunday School in the basement of the church in North Alabama where he first heard the story as a boy, he turned the word processor off. He could see the flannelboard on the wobbly easel. Stuck on it was the man who had fallen among thieves. Here came the priest, the Levite, and the Samaritan, in that order. One at a time, the arthritic fingers of Miss Pearl Boone placing them on the flannel and then removing them. He could see the seepage discoloring the plaster beneath the high window at ground level. But in the reality of the present moment there was still the lighted steeple of Memorial Presbyterian. George McKenna had come a long way from the hills of North Alabama. If you thought about it, he had come a lot farther than the mere 150 miles.

Unchanged, of course, was what happened on the road to Jericho. George believed that Miss Pearl Boone's flannelboard was as up-to-date as the 10 o'clock news that he had missed. And wasn't the story every bit as tailored for the congregation of Memorial as the pronouncement about rich men and heaven and camels and the eyes of needles? It tied right in, didn't it? It just might lay the groundwork for the other sermon later on.

So be it, George thought, and got up and touched the light switch beside the door and headed down the dark hall.

He stuck his head in Lindley's room. Window-paned moonlight defined the sculpture of her body beneath the covers. It shocked him that her head could be on the pillow and her feet that far down the bed. Where had he been? How could his daughter be eight already?

He went on down the hall. He was tired. But not too tired. Now that his course was set, now that his mind was free, his body reminded him it was still there, hungering.

There had been a time, early in his ministry, when he and Margaret had sacrificed their sexual desires on Saturday nights. He had figured that doing without was part of the prep. He still believed in the principle of sacrifice—how could he be a Christian and not? But he had come to a point where he saw that two bodies becoming one body was as spiritual as it was physical. That it was already the Lord's Day morning did not confuse the issue either. He would deny himself for only one reason. Margaret was probably asleep.

He approached the bed, peeling off his jersey.

Margaret was absolutely still.

He stepped out of his jeans, out of his Jockey shorts. Quietly.

"I'm not asleep," Margaret said.

❀ ❀ ❀

The anthem swelled and then subsided and was over. George, robed in black, stepped to the pulpit. The faces in the congregation blurred.

Now came the question that always confronted him at this point: *What in the world are you doing here?* The sword was in the stone and here he was, stumbling forth to do his stuff. Here he was once again, the matador facing the bravest of the bulls. Or, God forbid, the actor facing his audience.

What he was about was above those endeavors, was it not? Yet the thoughts never failed to attack. This morning, to make things worse, the actor didn't even have a script. Not beyond the text, which did happen to be longer than the ones he normally used, and thank God for that.

"Today I would like for us to consider our Lord's Parable about the Good Samaritan. This story is so familiar that it's possible to hear it without hearing it. Let us listen as we have never listened before. The Gospel of Luke, the tenth chapter, the twenty-fifth verse:

> On one occasion an expert in the law
> stood up to test Jesus. "Teacher," he
> asked, "what must I do to inherit eternal life?"
> "What is written in the Law?" he replied.

"How do you read it?"

He answered, "'Love the Lord your God with all your heart and with all your soul and with all your strength and with all your mind'; and, 'Love your neighbor as yourself.'"

"You have answered correctly," Jesus replied. "Do this and you will live."

But he wanted to justify himself, so he asked Jesus, "And who is my neighbor?"

In reply Jesus said: "A man was going down from Jerusalem to Jericho, when he fell into the hands of robbers. They stripped him of his clothes, beat him and went away, leaving him half dead. A priest happened to be going down the same road, and when he saw the man, he passed by on the other side. So too, a Levite, when he came to the place and saw him, passed by on the other side. But a Samaritan, as he traveled, came where the man was; and when he saw him, he took pity on him. He went to him and bandaged his wounds, pouring on oil and wine. Then he put the man on his own donkey, took him to an inn and took care of him. The next day he took out two silver coins and gave them to the innkeeper. 'Look after him,' he said, 'and when I return, I will reimburse you for any extra expense you may have.'

"Which of these three do you think was a

neighbor to the man who fell into the hands of robbers?"

The expert in the law replied, "The one who had mercy on him."

Jesus told him, "Go and do likewise."

Looking up from the Bible, George took in the three individuals that he preached to week after week. It was not that he considered them any more important than the rest of the congregation, but he had come to think of them as representing the whole. You couldn't talk to everybody at once. Not if you wanted to communicate on a personal level. Those three faces worked well as key targets—which was remarkable because each of them was a challenge, just as likely to nod with drowsiness as with agreement.

The silence had ended. He was preaching. Now to Harry Beckham, the bank president who was the leading elder, the man most responsible for George's call to this church. Now to Joel Scotney, the young man who had come to him several times for counsel in regard to homosexual temptations. Now to Rose Templeton, a cool blond widow, well off, well kept. Harry Beckham was in his usual place, down front on the left. Joel Scotney was in his, midships, over on the right. Rose Templeton reigned in her aisle seat near the back.

As he shifted his gaze from one to the other, he would scatter his attention widely enough to include everyone in a general way. But today the sermon seemed to direct itself, even with the three, more to one than the others. Like a river finding its path, it flowed where it would: toward Rose Templeton. It was a good thing she sat that far back. George was afraid the channeling might have been noticeable otherwise.

Rose Templeton was the first person he had called on after he became pastor of Memorial Presbyterian Church. Her husband, who had been in cotton in the days when the big money was there, and whose name still bannered a Front Street company, had died only a week before George's arrival. George remembered the poise with which she accepted his condolences. She chose not to spend his visit dwelling on her husband's memory. Nor on listening to the psalm he had prepared to read. She had, instead, given him the grand tour of the house. She had done it in a gracious, charming, even unpretentious way. She didn't have to be pretentious. The rooms were there, the antique rugs, the chandeliers, the portraits. The furniture was worn but of such a character one could not imagine that it ever stooped to a commercial showroom. The patina of the woods was genuine, not from an artificial stressing of the surfaces. It was all greatly appreciated—and shared as beauty—by this beautiful woman who had never had children and now had no husband.

George paused and took a sip of water from the little glass the deacon had placed on the shelf beneath the pulpit. It gave him a moment to take stock. To wing a sermon was not always to know where you were. Did he know where he was? Did he know where he was going? Yes, and he thought he might be doing all right.

"Why do I describe this parable as frightening? Because the Jesus who narrated the story to that lawyer is the same Jesus who will say to the people at the Last Judgment, 'It was I you met in the naked, the hungry, the imprisoned, and you did not help Me.' Someday the myriad of individuals represented by the priest and the Levite will say, 'Lord, when did we see You hungry or naked or sick?' This will be their chant as they are cast away.

"I pose a question. A crucial one. With whom do we identify in this parable? The lawyer was trying to test Jesus, trying to tangle Him in a theological debate. Jesus was ready for him when he asked, 'Who is my neighbor?' Ready with a story that brought lofty theology down to where it meets the road. Theology means nothing at all until it's fleshed out. If we identify with the lawyer, we need to know that.

"A man was going down from Jerusalem to Jericho. We don't know who this man was—he could be the man who checks you out at the quick market, who has a very generalized face. He could be the man who came around and sold you some manure to spread on your garden. He's probably not a member of your firm, or your club, and certainly not a member of your church.

CHAPTER ONE

"Whoever he is, he has met misfortune. And here comes a priest. He doesn't fail to *see* the wounded man. He sees him well enough to cross the street so that he won't have to look closely. Let's give him the benefit of the doubt. He's due to be in church at a certain hour, and he's already late. Even so, we don't wish to identify with *him*, do we?"

Rose Templeton stepped from the pew and scurried toward the back door. By the time George was able to fix his gaze upon her, she had disappeared into the narthex. So uncharacteristic of Rose Templeton, to *scurry*.

He was strangely disappointed. If Rose Templeton didn't return right away, she would miss the wrap-up. He didn't like to be judgmental, but somehow he had the feeling that she needed it more than any of the others.

"One thing for sure," he said, "we can't identify with the Samaritan. If we are honest with ourselves—if we are honest with God—we must identify with those who crossed to the other side of the road. We must confess that sometimes Jesus just isn't all that attractive. You see, it's only with that kind of confession that we can begin to look at Him as He hangs on the cross, 'despised and rejected of men.'"

George was heading for the finish and he thought he might be doing all right. But Rose Templeton had not returned.

❀ ❀ ❀

Laura's voice over the intercom: "Mrs. Lambie is calling for an appointment. She would like to see you today if possible. She says it's very important."

The day was just beginning and George was reading his mail. He glanced at the desk calendar. It was going to be a better Friday than last Friday because his sermon was ready and he had room to breathe, but the calendar was crammed.

"There goes lunch," he said to Laura.

"But you're supposed to meet Mr. Ashton at Lulu Grille at twelve."

That pleasant voice of Laura's helped to balance the frustration.

He said, "Thanks for the reminder. I didn't have that down. So what do we do?"

"Are you asking me?"

"I'm asking the Lord."

"Oh."

"Tell you what. Tell Mrs. Lambie to come in at five. I can hang around."

❀ ❀ ❀

Among the lunch crowd at Lulu Grille, George spotted five members of Memorial Presbyterian. His flock was "on the scene" in East Memphis. It did not surprise him that they would frequent this place. He liked it himself. Tucked away in an alcove, seeming to retreat from the shops that faced the parking lot, the quiet bistro sported lace curtains and starchy-aproned waiters. It was about as classy as one would want for lunch, unless one wanted pure show.

The man across the table, who was footing the bill today, was not a member of Memorial Presbyterian. George knew little about Robert Ashton except that he was an attorney who had been visiting the church on and off for months. The purpose of this lunch, Robert Ashton had warned, was to put some questions to him. The meal was nearly over and the questions were still coming.

"—and you believe that the Scriptures are to be taken literally?"

George tore off a scrap of French bread, touched it to the black bean soup and then popped it into his mouth. You could remove the boy from Alabama, but you couldn't remove Alabama from the boy. It occurred to him that Robert Ashton might think the same was true in regard to the answer that was about to come out.

"Yes."

"A straight question, a straight answer."

"I don't argue for a six-day creation," he said, " though I do personally believe that's how it was. Is that where you get hung up?"

"That's one place, but it's the Virgin Birth I'm thinking about."

"Good. I'm glad you're thinking about that. Some people never do."

"I find myself drawn to your sermons, but I realize they don't hold water, any of them, unless it's true." Robert Ashton was about to pierce the last veal medallion with his fork, but he didn't. He seemed to have lost his appetite all of a sudden. "The thing is, I can't make myself believe it."

"At least you're honest and consistent. You'd be surprised at the number of people who are willing to accept a virgin born Savior but not a virgin born universe. As if God could perform one miracle but not another."

"All this," Robert Ashton said, "and we haven't even talked about the Resurrection."

"That's a biggie," George acknowledged.

Alice Lambie was wearing her hot pink jogging suit. Her face was flushed, almost a match for the suit. Had George not seen the Cadillac pull up, he might have thought she had jogged the two miles from Holly Park Drive. Somewhere in her late forties or early fifties, a model of health, she probably jogged farther than that every day. But no—it was obvious that the color in Alice Lambie's face was a sign she was upset.

George had risen to greet her. When she sank into the chair, he sat on the edge of his desk. "How's Ed?" he asked. George's way was always to cover generalities first and put people at ease.

"Ed's fine."

"He beat me in handball, you know."

Clearly, Alice Lambie wasn't interested in her husband's handball. She said, "That sermon last Sunday—"

George waited.

"That sermon—no, I'll get right to the point—"

Again, George waited.

"You've got to do something about Rose Templeton. She took that sermon too seriously."

"I'm at a loss here," George said. "Mrs. Templeton left before the service was over."

"Yes, I know," Alice Lambie said.

"Fill me in." George was really curious. Often he had to pretend curiosity in order to be nice. Today it was the genuine thing.

"No one has come to you with this?"

"No one."

"Maybe I'm the only person who knows. I certainly hope so. We've been the closest of friends since grade school at St. Mary's. I can't bear the thought of Rose being talked about. I come to you with it only because of the part you played in what has happened."

"Which is—"

The story began to unravel. Rose Templeton on the way to church last Sunday had stopped at Seessel's supermarket for a pound of coffee. As she was walking back to the car, this man came toward her for a handout. She shooed him off and got behind the wheel as quickly as possible. Driving away, she saw him sit down on the pavement with his back against the dumpster.

George raced ahead of the narrative. The encounter with the panhandler was in Rose Templeton's mind during the sermon. Alice Lambie caught up with George's correct guess, and from there she took him where he would never have ventured.

Rose Templeton left the church and went back to Seessel's parking lot to see if the man was there. He was, but barely. A customer must have reported him and the manager had come out to send him on his way. "Rose did have the good sense to wait until the manager had gone back inside. I mean, what would he have thought? She invited—this—*man*—into her car. She drove home and invited him into the house and prepared a Sunday dinner for him. She has never prepared a Sunday dinner for anyone that I know of. She always eats out on Sunday. Not last Sunday. She prepared a Sunday dinner and sat down at the table with this person. Not the kitchen, mind you. The dining room. She made a point of telling me that."

George could feel a smile playing at the corner of his lips and he didn't know what to do with it. "This is extraordinary," he heard himself whispering.

"Don't smile, Pastor. This is serious. We're not talking about something that happened in the Bible. We're talking about real life, if you can believe it. Get ready for this. She invited him to stay for supper. To make a long story short, that person is still there, sleeping in the guest room."

The smile left of its own accord. George placed his palms together and his fingertips touched his chin. It was at that moment not so much an attitude of prayer as a gesture of deep thought. But it was an empty gesture. George did not know exactly what to think.

"She told me all of this on the phone. *Offered* it. I told her quite plainly what I thought and I realized I was talking to a brick wall. She is not the Rose Templeton I've known all of these years. What will people think? The appearances!"

"What people think," George said, "is not the important thing. The important thing—"

"Pastor, the danger!"

George realized that he was fumbling.

His palms were still together, his fingertips touching his chin.

CHAPTER 2

$\mathcal{W}$hat is it?" Margaret asked.

"What is what?"

"Look, I've been married to you for ten years. I know when something's troubling you."

They had finished supper. Lindley had been excused from the table to do her homework, which consisted of writing a poem about winter. Margaret was clearing away the dishes and George was just sitting there with one elbow where his plate had been.

He said, "I just wasn't that hungry, that's all."

Margaret returned to the table and sat opposite him. "Is it something we can talk about? If it isn't, I'll shut up." She brushed at a crumb.

"I have to pay a call on Rose Templeton sometime soon. How would you like to accompany me?"

"What kind of call?"

"Aye, there's the rub—"

Lindley came in and wanted to know if snowman was one or two words. Neither of her parents was sure.

Instead of sending her to the dictionary, George suggested that she think of something other than a snowman to write about. "I'll bet everybody writes a poem about a snowman. Why don't you try to think of something different?"

She considered that for a moment. OK—she would. She disappeared.

George proceeded to tell Margaret what Alice Lambie had told him. There was much a minister had to keep zipped, but this was something he could discuss with his wife. He watched Margaret's eyes widen as she listened. The dismay remained on her face when he had finished, and she sat there in silence.

They both sat there in silence.

Finally Margaret said, "You must be very careful how you handle this."

"How would you like to accompany me on the call? I think this is one of those times when—"

Margaret was shaking her head from side to side. "This is your little red wagon," she said. In her voice was a touch of gentleness, but it didn't weaken her refusal.

"You see the innate problem," George said.

"You're in the position of saying that it's dangerous to take the Bible seriously."

"And I can't say that."

"No, but whatever you do say, that will be the logical inference."

Lindley had come back. She was pumping for ideas.

George suggested that she write a poem about a fire blazing in a fireplace.

"But we don't have a fire," his daughter said. "We don't even have a fireplace."

Margaret told Lindley that Daddy was thinking about his own childhood.

"Poems come out of the imagination," George said. He drew Lindley to his side and embraced her. "They don't have to be about something real."

Margaret asked her, "What is your own very favorite thing about winter?"

Lindley looked at the ceiling.

George let it go and got back to *his* quandary. But he was still in both worlds. Enough to say, "When you think of it, just write something about it and make it rhyme."

As though from a distance, he heard Lindley declare that her favorite thing about winter was seeing her breath on cold mornings.

"That's ve-r-r-y good!" Margaret said.

"It's like a little fog that comes out of your mouth and blows away to nothing," Lindley said.

"You've almost got a poem right there," George said. He had not deserted his little girl and he wanted her to know it.

"My teacher says it doesn't have to rhyme," she tossed over her shoulder as she left the room.

Margaret reached across the table. Her fingertips met his. "Don't sweat it," she said. "I can't imagine that the man is still there. Besides—even if he is—your involvement in this is *so* indirect. Perhaps you should let well enough alone."

The telephone rang at dawn. It was not the ideal way to begin a Saturday. George's protesting moans could not quell the disturbance. Trying to prepare himself for the kind of message a pastor might expect at such an hour, he rolled over and fumbled for the receiver.

His father's voice. George saw him standing at the telephone in the narrow hall, an old cardigan on, probably misbuttoned. If it was a normal morning in that little bungalow in Florence, Alabama, the lights had been on since 4:30 and his father had been sitting with his coffee and his Bible. He never seemed to grasp that other people did not rise that early.

"Son," he said, "I've been having strange premonitions recently."

"What kind of premonitions, Dad?"

"That I won't be here forever."

"None of us will be here forever, Dad."

The conversation didn't amount to much more than

that, except that George kept asking if he was having chest pains and his father kept saying he wasn't.

In a couple of hours George found himself on the road to Alabama. He wanted to check on things and be sure. He might be driving 150 miles just to have a cup of coffee, but that was all right. He was glad it was close enough to get there and back in one day, tomorrow being Sunday. He had canceled the golf game with Harry Beckham. That was all right too. It was too cold to chase a golf ball around. Margaret wasn't coming along because she had to take Lindley to her piano lesson.

Although time was a priority, George was sort of glad there wasn't an interstate between Memphis and Florence. He always needed time for the transition. On an interstate it would be zoom and he would be there, and it would be disconcerting to find the past no farther away than that. Passing though the small towns gave him time to get his bearings.

His father had been a widower for seven years now, but the house had the same air as when his mother was alive. It was the case of a man who had never lifted a hand in the house, now dusting and vacuuming and not doing a bad job of it. Meals had changed—George suspected that his father ate straight from cans most of the time—but, beyond that, little was different. The rooms were still the rooms George had grown up in. Not a chair had budged. The collection of candlesticks continued to march across the mantel. The ferns in the dining room window might be a new generation, but who could tell?

When George nosed his Buick up to the rear of his father's Ford pickup, his father came out of the house and down the porch steps. Nothing unusual about that, either. Since his father had sold the hardware store, it seemed he was always waiting at the window when George came home. Today, especially, it was good to see the old man in action. It was good to observe the regular pace and to feel the fist that punched at his middle. He thought about Lindley's poem, for it was good to see the little fogs of breath, of life, that came out of his father's mouth and disappeared in the winter sunlight.

"You're a good boy," his father said.

"Not really," George said. "But I did want to check up on you."

"I'm feeling much better now, thank you."

They went inside. George followed his father into the kitchen. Coffee was *perking*. Not making but *perking*. That in itself—the very smell—was worth the trip.

"You're not getting signals you should talk with Doc about?"

A thorough scoff. "I think I just needed to see my boy."

Mixed with George's relief and the pleasant anticipation of the coffee was a feeling of exasperation. But then it had been six months—no—nine months since he had come down for a visit. The exasperation eased. That left the guilt.

They sipped their coffee and talked about whatever the old man brought up. George was tempted to ask his opinion of the Rose Templeton problem. He decided not to mention it. The most constructive counsel from his father had always been by example, not by mouth, and that kind of guidance was not possible in a situation like this. Nor called for. Margaret was right—it was *his* little red wagon.

The only person in Florence whose opinion he might seek, although it was somewhat fanciful to even think of it, was Miss Pearl Boone, who, with her flannel board, had introduced him to the Parable of the Good Samaritan in the first place.

He asked if she was still living.

"Last I heard, she was still holding on."

They drove past the hardware store. They did not stop. Those memories did not apply at the moment. Farther on, they drove past the church that was no longer there. The new one, the one that didn't look like a church at all, was down a block and not on their way.

On the screened porch of Heavenly Sunshine Home a coterie of rocking chairs sat in stillness, in conversational groupings, as though remembering summer. Inside, at the end of the hall that led straight back, was a brightly lighted recreation room. It was as close to summer as you could get on a day like that. Miss Pearl Boone seemed to know it. She was rocking contentedly.

"Miss Pearl, do you remember me?" George asked.

She smiled and nodded her head and kept on rocking.

"Remember that old Sunday School room in the basement?"

She kept smiling. Nodding. Rocking.

There would be no counsel here, George realized.

His father said, "Pearlie, don't you remember my boy?"

George stared at the profound vacancy. He was struck with a sorrow that went much deeper than the immediate disappointment.

It was almost four when he left his father's house and headed for the first of the bridges he would cross on his way back to Memphis.

Rose Templeton was not in her spot the next morning. That was almost unheard of. If she wasn't on a cruise or something, Rose Templeton could be expected to be in church on Sunday. George was inclined to attribute her faithful attendance to rigid tradition and not spirituality. Nevertheless, she was always there and that was more than you could say for some of the members.

But she wasn't there that morning.

Alice Lambie was, with her head cocked slightly to

one side as she listened to the sermon. George detected in her eyes the same challenge with which she had confronted him in his office on Friday. He noticed that occasionally her head turned and she threw a glance toward the rear of the church, toward Rose Templeton's pew. Whether she did it to see if her friend had come in late or to emphasize to him that she was absent, he wasn't sure. He had to block it all out to keep his mind on the sermon he was preaching. It was good the sermon was prepared and down on paper and not like last Sunday.

At the dinner table, over spaghetti, he asked Margaret if he should telephone first or just show up.

"You're going this afternoon?"

"Thought I would."

"I don't think it will amount to anything at all. I say the man's long gone and she has a bad cold or something."

"You haven't answered my question, sweetheart."

"I think just show up is best."

As George drove toward Carriage Way, he began to resent what God had gotten him into. He always tried to be honest with God. He might as well be, he figured, since God could look inside the heart anyway. *I hate this business of having to backtrack on what you've put forth. But what else can I do? I'm caught. Alice Lambie is right, this is real life in some way that the parable is not.*

There were no sidewalks on Carriage Way. The lawns ran down to the blacktop. Now in winter they had the same cared-for look they had in summer when the Zoysia was green and lush. The houses sat back in confident repose, achieving attitudes that bound them together as kindred statements despite the physical distances between them and the variety of their architectural styles. The miscellany had evolved over the years preceding World War II and was not the result, so common nowadays even in moneyed neighborhoods, of a single builder's studied modifications.

Reigning between a Tudor manor and something tiled and Spanish, the Templeton residence was one of those monuments to the Old South that Memphians never seemed to tire of: the veranda, the columns, the chimneys, the fanlight above the door. Although one could picture a black butler serving mint juleps on a summer afternoon, the severe good taste of the architect had prevented a cliché. Remembering a family dressed in white playing croquet in front of a similar house in the Florence of his boyhood, George stepped out of the Buick and onto the brick walk that curved toward the entrance. Here he was, and he still was not sure exactly how to broach the subject that had prompted his call.

Rose Templeton answered the bell. "Why, Pastor, what a pleasant surprise," she said, inviting him in. She was wearing a tailored shirt, with a little crisscross ribbon tie that matched her navy blue slacks.

"I think it's about time you call me George, Mrs. Templeton."

"I think it's about time you call me Rose."

"How are things going, Rose?"

"Top notch. How are things going with you, George?" She took his coat and lay it across one of the attending chairs in the hall.

Before following her into the sitting room, George sent his gaze up the stairs and along the banistered passageway above the hall. Faintly came the sound of a shower, and not so faintly, the sound of a man singing.

"Don't tell me," Rose Templeton said, laughing, "that I miss my first Sunday in years and you chase me down for a scolding." She motioned to a chair.

"Now you know I wouldn't do a thing like that," George said, sitting down.

"How is that lovely wife of yours?"

"Margaret's fine."

"And your little girl?"

"Lindley's fine too."

"A charming child."

"Why, thank you. We think so."

"I'm sure you do."

"Mrs. Templeton—Rose—"

"Let me help you," she said. She was sitting on the love seat, leaning slightly forward, a kindness in her eyes. "Did Alice Lambie send you to check up on me?"

The hurdle was crossed. With a sense of relief, George proceeded from there. "Mrs. Lambie is concerned about you," he said.

"Alice has a nose a mile long."

"It's only natural that your friend is uneasy. She's worried about—"

"Appearances," Rose Templeton said.

"She's worried about more than appearances."

"I *know* Alice Lambie."

George said, "She's worried about your safety."

Rose Templeton got up and walked to the window. She stood there, looking out. Then she turned and faced him again. "I doubt that the Gospel has ever been *safe*."

That remark, had it come from his super spiritual roommate in seminary, would have been ho-hum. Had it come from his own mouth, it would not have been ho-hum at all but neither would it have surprised him. It was strong wording, and he knew even at that moment that someday he would use it himself. But this was Rose Templeton, whom he might have put at the top of the list of the materialistic people in his church. From her, standing there at the window with her Jaguar visible on the back drive and the portrait of some ancestor gazing down on the old and lustrous Steinway, the remark achieved astounding power. Her almost casual tone seemed to intensify it somehow. He doubted if his delivery could ever match it, no matter what fervor he mustered.

George sat there listening to the echo within him. He went from feeling flushed to feeling pale.

Very carefully, without going against what she had

said, he began to try to talk sense to her. At one point he
said, "Mrs. Templeton—Rose—you are a reasonable
woman. We—all of us—must keep a balance—"

The woman sat down. Not on the love seat this time
but on the piano bench, which was nearer to where he
sat. "George, I come from a long line of Presbyterians—
reasonable, balanced Presbyterians. I occupy the same
end of the same pew my great-grandmother did. Not in
the same building of course—it was torn down after the
congregation flew to East Memphis. I'm there Sunday in
and Sunday out—"

"You're very faithful, I know that," George interject-
ed.

"—and I'm not there on principle only. I listen. I've
listened all these years. But I confess I never heard any of
it before that sermon of yours last Sunday. I don't mean
to imply that you and your predecessors have not presented it. It is I who have flunked the Gospel."

George reminded Rose Templeton that the Parable of
the Good Samaritan was not an equation of the Gospel.
G-o-s-p-e-l meant good news. The good news was this:
Christ died for our sins, and by His grace we are set free.
The parable was not second-rate Scripture, but to think
of it as the Gospel—well—

"Either it all holds together or it doesn't hold at all,"
she said flatly.

Without waiting for his response, she went on with
her personal account of how this man had approached

her in the parking lot at Seessel's, how she had left church early, and returned to find him still there. "My intention was to take him to McDonald's and pay for anything he wanted, complete the transaction myself, and therefore preclude his using the money for booze or whatever, but do you know what? I couldn't do it. Not after your sermon. Do you understand?"

"I do," George admitted. "Yet I think it behooves us to make the distinction between a hungry man and a wounded man. The man in the parable was a wounded man. The man who approached you—"

"Was a wounded man," Rose Templeton said. "I made the mistake of looking into his eyes."

"The Samaritan tended the man's wounds and took him to an inn where he received care and shelter. He did not take him home. Your charity is noble, but it's not precisely called for in the parable. For the sake of your safety, Rose, I must point out that the precedent simply is not there."

"I made the mistake of looking," she reflected. "On occasion I have been taken to task—by a good and straightforward friend—for not speaking to people who have less than I do. I have resented that judgment. But I no longer plead innocent. I think that people of my— how shall I say this?—people of my advantages—yes—I think that we tend not to see other people. It's not that we set out to be haughty. We just don't see them. We just don't look."

George realized he was getting nowhere. For something to say, he said, "I had thought you might bring this individual to the service this morning." He punctuated the sentence with the best smile he could come up with. Secretly he was glad she hadn't, and he hated himself for feeling that way.

"I invited him. You can be sure of that. I pushed him to wear one of my husband's suits—several of them have hung in the closet all this time—I've never been able to give them up, silly as that sounds. He got as far as trying a suit on—it did fit—but then he backed out. He said he just wouldn't feel comfortable there. I could understand that, so I got ready and was about to go out the door when I questioned my priorities. I decided to stay home and make pancakes for a man who likes pancakes. Birdie has left me—she very much disapproved of my guest—but these boxed mixes practically prepare themselves. You will be happy to know, George, that I've been saying grace at our meals—aloud. I've never done that before in my life."

George rose to leave. He commended the woman for the work of charity in which she was involved. He went so far as to say "the work of charity to which God has called you." Having done that, he fell back to his previous position and urged her toward a different arrangement. "This is all well and good, but the time comes when a return to normalcy is in order."

She said, "Wasn't it Nicodemus who asked how a person could return to the womb?"

George was up against a brick wall. This was conversion as he had never seen it, conversion as he had never heard of.

The sound of the shower had ceased during the visit, and with it the singing.

As the two of them were passing the stairs on the way to the door, Rose Templeton paused and touched George's arm. She looked up in the direction of the banistered passageway. For a moment it seemed that she might summon the man they had been discussing, but she must have thought better of it. She made no move to introduce George to her unseen visitor. Which of them to protect from the other, he could not be sure.

Rose Templeton held his coat for him. She apologized for not offering him something to drink. "We had so much on our minds, didn't we?"

❈ ❈ ❈

On Tuesday night George and Margaret bumped into Joel Scotney in the crowded lobby of the Orpheum, during intermission.

"Is this your first *Les Mis*?" Joel asked.

"Hardly," George quipped.

"How about number three?" Margaret said.

George, vaguely wondering how Joel was getting along with his temptations, said, "You can call this 'theatre' all you want—*Les Mis* is reality. This is the battle. Here is evil, here is good. Here is sin, here is redemption."

"Is he preaching?" Joel said to Margaret, with a nudge and a wink.

"Sounds like it to me," Margaret said.

"Seriously," George said, "this is grace in the raw, played out in the streets of revolutionary Paris. It's the same Gospel, you know. Paris, Memphis, Timbuktu—"

"You *are* preaching, "Margaret said.

"Let him go," Joel said. "I need a dose."

"Sorry, that's it for now." George pointed toward the rest rooms. "I was heading in that direction."

"I think I'd better take advantage also," his wife said, and was on her way, squeezing through.

George hung with Joel for a moment. Strangely, the thickness of chatting humanity surrounding them created a little island of privacy. "How are things with you, Joel?"

"I'm still struggling," Joel said, matter of factly.

George thought for a moment. He sent a fist toward Joel's stomach. It stopped just shy of its mark. His father's kind of action but without impact. It gave George time to come up with something worth saying. "If you're struggling," he said, "it means you're alive. The dead—the spiritually dead as well as the physically dead—don't struggle. There's no tension for them. Tension is a sign of life, my friend. Remember that."

The men's line was not as long as the women's. When George came out of the rest room, he stood at the foot of the left stairway, where he and Margaret were in the habit of reconnecting. He saw Joel Scotney, apparently dateless, ascending the stairway on the right.

The twin stairways turned to face each other on the mezzanine level. The upward flow was increasing now, and framed between the flights the downstairs crowd was beginning to drift toward the doors beneath. George caught sight of Rose Templeton just before she disappeared through the center door. She seemed to be with a another woman. The best he could tell, the recipient of her charity was not accompanying her. Although George would not have expected her to bring him to something like this, you never knew. He would not have expected any of it. The glimpse of her without some questionable shadow wearing her husband's suit was heartening.

The lights blinked.

"Let's hurry," Margaret said, approaching.

George reached for her hand and they too made for their seats, ready for more of the music and passion of *Les Misérables*.

❀ ❀ ❀

George pressed the button. He was about to ask Laura to get Rose Templeton on the phone. He changed his mind. He went out to Laura's desk and thumbed through the little Ferris wheel of cards, got the number and went back into his office to place the call himself.

A man's voice answered. George asked to speak with Mrs. Templeton.

Mrs. Templeton, he learned from the monotone, was out shopping.

"My name is George McKenna. I'm Mrs. Templeton's pastor." George waited for the voice on the other end to speak again.

"OK," it came. A certain caution.

"And your name?"

"Dusty."

"Your last name?"

Sort of a laugh, under the breath. "I always figured with a handle like Dusty you didn't need more than that."

George wanted to be genial. "*No-o-o-o*—everybody needs a full name. Most of the Dustys I've known or heard about had the surname of Rhodes. Is that it? Did I guess it?"

"No. It's Case."

"Dusty Case. Well, Mr. Case—uh—"

"I'm Mrs. Templeton's houseguest." *If anyone calls, you may identify yourself as my houseguest.* George could hear Rose Templeton instructing him.

"Yes—and that's very nice of Mrs. Templeton, isn't it? She's a lovely lady, a lovely Christian lady, isn't she?"

"Yes, she is, Brother McKenna."

The "Brother" struck a chord. Dusty probably had a background in Baptist or Pentecostal traditions.

George said, "Just call me George."

"I think I better stick with Brother McKenna."

"In Presbyterian circles we usually go with 'Mister' but it's no big deal, no big deal one way or the other."

"All right."

George heard himself deliver nervous laughter. He must stop rambling.

"Dusty," he said, getting down to business, "Mrs. Templeton's friends and I are as concerned about you as she is." Such a fuzzy line between the truth and a lie, he thought, and he winced. "I would like to help you if I can. Help you get on your feet, get a new start. We have Christian organizations here in Memphis that you might not be aware of. Maybe you and I could have lunch and I could give you a list of contacts."

"I know some of those organizations." The monotone again.

"My church supports some fine ones. Some really good things are going on nowadays. You been in Memphis long?"

"All my life except for Nam."

"In what part of town did you grow up?" George said.

"Near the fairgrounds. What they used to call Cooper-Young. I bet you never heard of that district."

"You're wrong about that. We parked down that way last fall when we went to the fair. That's right—too cheap to pay the fee for parking on the grounds."

"Hope you didn't get your car stolen."

"No. I'm happy to report that it was right there when we got back. I took it as an answer to prayer, though."

"It used to be a decent neighborhood," Dusty said. "I lived there with my grandmother. She was the only family I had."

"Still living?"

"I don't know. I doubt it. I broke all connections a long time ago."

"That's very sad."

"I guess so."

George said, "About that lunch—"

"Brother McKenna, Mrs. Templeton's driving up. I better get off and help her with the groceries. Want me to call her to the phone?"

"Uh—no." George had called to find out if Rose Templeton had followed his counsel. The answer was obvious. "Go on and help her with the groceries. We'll talk later, you and I, about that lunch."

🌸 🌸 🌸

"What's the latest on Rose Templeton?" Margaret asked, crawling into bed.

George was already there. It was not a good time to discuss the latest on Rose Templeton. George was keyed for something else entirely.

"Nothing has changed, last I heard," he said.

"Don't forget that one week from tonight is Lindley's piano recital."

George tried to turn his groan into a sigh, but he was too late.

"That's not fair," Margaret said.

"Wild horses couldn't keep me away."

"Promise?"

"Promise."

Between the Rose Templeton situation and the prospect of another piano recital, the pastor of Memorial Presbyterian Church lost the peak of his ardor and snuggled up to his wife for quiet and for warmth and for nothing else.

Harry Beckham, after the regular monthly meeting of the session, cornered George privately. Harry wore the presidency of his bank and his honcho position on the board of elders of Memorial Presbyterian with a casualness that allowed him to horse around without ever losing his essential posture. Tonight he wasn't horsing around.

"I understand that Alice Lambie came to you before she came to me," he said.

"Oh, dear," George breathed, knowing what was up.

George had never heard those words come out of his

CHAPTER TWO

mouth before. Not that he could remember. They sounded effeminate.

"George, her concerns are valid. Something's got to be done about this thing with Rose Templeton. In one sense, it's not our business—but then again, it is. When we come right down to it, it's *your* business."

Having said that, Harry Beckham was ready to spar.

Once again George and Robert Ashton were lunching at Lulu Grille.

Today they had met by accident. George of course, if someone pressed him, would have said there were no accidents with God. They had pulled up in the parking lot at the same time. Hailing each other, they had learned that neither of them was meeting someone else.

Now they sat at a table beside the lace-curtained window and talked of this and that as they waited for their sandwiches. George wondered if he should introduce the subject of the Resurrection again or wait until it came up naturally. He advised himself not to push ahead of the Spirit. He observed how far Robert Ashton's build and spiffy suit missed the pot and the rumpledness of the old stereotypical southern lawyer. Finding out that he was a defense attorney, George asked how he dealt with the question of representing someone he suspected was guilty—didn't that present a moral dilemma?

George's mind was somewhat divided as he listened to Robert Ashton's answer, and that was hardly fair since he had plied for the information. But something in the sunlight filtering through the lace drew his attention to the little courtyard outside the window where, hidden in the cold, a different season was waiting to be. Only a week ago the chairs and tables out there had registered as incongruities, and now, though still empty, they appeared as believable promises. Before long, no doubt, Lindley's homework would be to write a poem about spring. At the thought of Lindley, George was shamed by his lack of anticipation in regard to the upcoming recital. He made a vow—this one to himself, and to God—that he would not miss it.

Robert Ashton was saying, "—and with our country's legal system—"

George said, "I know that everyone should be presumed innocent until proven guilty—but—I know that in some cases, if I were personally involved, I'd have difficulty with that."

"—each individual is allowed his day in court—duly represented—"

"True." George saw the sandwiches coming.

"—so, with clear conscience, I can defend the accused—on his or her own terms, whether he or she is guilty or not—and expect justice to be served."

"So be it," George said, smiling over the stuffed croissant.

He had taken only one bite when the hostess came to the table. "Are you George McKenna?" she inquired. "You have a telephone call."

George followed her to the hostess station.

It was Laura. "I hate to bother you at lunch, but we just received word and I thought you'd want to know—"

George waited. What was wrong with his secretary's voice?

The next thing he knew, she was telling him that Rose Templeton had been murdered.

He stood there with the receiver against his ear. For one instant, for one merciful instant, he was absolutely blank. Who was Rose Templeton and how could she have been murdered? He didn't know people who were murdered.

CHAPTER 3

"I'm her pastor," George explained at the door.

The officer was a purist. "Was her pastor," he said, with remarkable dispassion.

"Uh—yes."

They stood aside as the stretcher bearing the sheeted body came out. Something told George to extend his hand and touch the sheet, but he resisted. It seemed his duty to give some kind of blessing, but at this point what blessing was there to give? He felt totally unequipped.

He was allowed entrance. As soon as he was inside the house, he realized he didn't know exactly why he was there.

He asked someone, "How—?"

The answer took some digging. In time he found out that Rose Templeton had received a bullet from a revolver that was registered in her own name. The revolver was discovered nearby. Suicide? Hardly. From the evidence, there had been some kind of fight.

"Where was she found?

"In her bedroom."

The stairway was taped off. George had no desire to go up, tape or no tape.

Talk volleyed between a man downstairs and one above. Against that background, a black female officer came up and asked George if he knew anything about the man who had been living there. George told her about Dusty Case, told her all he knew without bringing his sermon into it. He learned that Alice Lambie had discovered the body and called the police.

"She was still here when I arrived," the woman said. "She was full of talk about this character—"

George could imagine.

"—but she didn't know his name and couldn't give a description. His name is Case?"

"That's what he said."

"Does he go by anything besides Dusty?"

"Not that I know of."

"What age would you say?"

"I never saw him."

"You can't give us a description?"

"I only talked with him on the phone."

"If you had to guess his age—did he sound young? Old?"

"Uh—between thirty-five and fifty, maybe. Somewhere in that range."

"Listen, I'll be thirty-five next week. Do you realize you just lumped me with people fifteen years older than I am? I'm not ready for this."

"Don't worry," he said. "I hit thirty-five last fall and it didn't hurt much."

The attempt at levity fell flat. Rose Templeton was still dead and George McKenna was still a factor.

His head was pounding as he turned off of Carriage Way and aimed the Buick toward home. He wanted to talk with Margaret before he talked with anyone else. He just might lay his head on her lap and bawl. He thought he would feel better if he could do that.

Not until the church came into view did he think about the funeral to be conducted.

"I can't do it," he said aloud, pulling up beside Margaret's Volvo. "Someone else will have to officiate."

He repeated those statements to his wife as his arms went around her. She had already heard about the death. He dropped his head to her shoulder. He would forgo the lap and the tears, but some of the tears came anyway.

In time she withdrew and looked at him and said, "You've got to be kidding. Not do her funeral? *Why not?*"

"I just can't."

"George, this is not called for."

"The whole thing was not called for," he said.

Margaret took her keys from the hook beside the

kitchen door and disappeared. The Volvo purred. It was time to pick up Lindley at school.

George went to the telephone to call Laura. He stood there trying to put his thoughts together before lifting the receiver. He would tell her he was coming down with a bug and she must get in touch with Bill Taylor. As assistant to the pastor, Bill would have to assume all responsibilities in regard to the Templeton funeral. Bill got off easy most of the time, but this was one of those times when he would have to take over. Bill was a capable man. He could handle it. Be good experience for him. He wouldn't put it that way to Laura, of course. Not exactly.

He lifted the receiver and then replaced it. He couldn't make the call. He couldn't go that far. Perhaps he could find himself in his study. He was moving in that direction, but he passed the door and had to turn back. He got down on his knees, his elbows on the chair. He found that he couldn't pray. He wasn't used to praying on his knees. Maybe that was it, and maybe it was time to do so. He waited.

My God, my God, how did this happen?

That was the only prayer that came. And was it really a prayer? Could a question be a prayer? Yes. But whether or not an answer would come was another matter, of course.

From far away, the telephone rang.

He pushed himself up. There was no telephone in the

study—he'd had it removed long ago. His legs felt strange as he walked down the hall. Was it the result of kneeling? Had he been on his knees that long? But it was weakness, not a pain. Perhaps he was coming down with a bug after all. That thought was almost pleasant.

Alice Lambie was on the line. "Yes," he said, he had heard the news. He had been to the house himself, must have arrived shortly after she left. Did she know if Rose Templeton had any family at all?

"One sister," Alice Lambie said. "I assume she'll be making the arrangements. Poor, poor Rose."

"This is very awkward of me," George said, "but I seem to be coming down with a bug—a *violent* bug of some kind."

"I can understand," Alice Lambie said.

"I'm turning the service over to Bill Taylor. He'll do a fine job. Bill's a fine man."

Alice Lambie wasn't ready to hang up. "I hope you told the police everything you know about the man she had taken in."

"You can be sure I did. Everything I know."

"They *must* find him. He *must not* go unpunished."

"The thing is, I don't know that much. I did talk with him on the phone, but I never met him. Do you know if his problem was booze?"

"On that level, what other problem is there?"

That was not a good way to say it, George reflected. He knew what she meant though, and let it go at that.

Before he could terminate the conversation, Alice Lambie's tone suddenly lost its grief and found an edge of pride. "I was right, wasn't I?"

🐚 🐚 🐚

He was talking to his secretary when Margaret and Lindley came in. "On second thought," he said, "I'll call Bill myself. That's better form, I think. But if you would get in touch with Harry Beckham and advise him that I'm down with a bug."

"Don't you worry about a thing," Laura said.

Margaret, who had heard him, stood there looking at him, shaking her head.

"I *am* sick," he said when he was off the phone. "My legs are like water."

"Daddy," Lindley said, "why would somebody want to murder that lady?"

The pastor of Memorial Presbyterian Church drew his daughter to himself and hugged her. "I don't know, honey. I just don't know."

He called Bill Taylor. "You're at the helm," he told him.

"No problem," Bill Taylor assured him.

George went into the bathroom off the back hall—he went to that one because it was the closest—and locked the door and sat down on the lid of the toilet. He didn't want to talk with Margaret.

❀ ❀ ❀

The murder of Rose Templeton was the first item on the 10 o'clock news on all the local stations. George flicked from one channel to the other, feeling that he was missing whatever might be on the other channel, and ultimately feeling that he had missed something important in the act of switching. The victim's social standing was the main focus, from what he picked up, but the reporter on the last channel did trail off with a comment about a search for a suspected itinerant.

"This is the first time in ten years of marriage," Margaret said, "that we have stooped so low as to take our telephone off the hook."

"I think that's a pretty good record," George said.

"Okay, so you feel entangled—personally entangled— I don't think anybody but Mrs. Lambie is onto that. I've no doubt that Rose Templeton's other friends in the church are wanting to talk with their pastor—with the pastor that you *are*, whether you like it or not right now."

George turned off the television set and said nothing.

After a while, Margaret put aside her needlepoint-in-progress. "I think I'll go on to bed," she said, and was gone.

George reached up and turned off the lamp beside his chair. The light coming from around the corner in the hallway sculpted the shapes in the family room with a vagueness that George found oddly comforting. Escape of any kind was attractive on this particular night. Sleep would be a blessing, and maybe the world would fall into order overnight and he would be able to deal with things objectively tomorrow.

He knew the scenario that awaited him if he went to bed. He would lie there and toss. Better to stay right here and let sleep catch him unaware. On the paneled wall hung a framed photograph, too dim to make out, of himself and the old pastor who preached the sermon at his ordination. The photograph might be indistinct, but the memory of that sermon wasn't. Now one part of it came to George so clearly that he could hear that gravelly voice and see those piercing old eyes that looked down at him in the front pew.

"George McKenna, if you're going to be a servant of the Word, then it will be necessary for you to be broken up in little pieces and distributed just like the bread of Communion. You're about to get the hands laid on you. Do you know where that practice started? Not in the New Testament. Back in the Old Testament when the they laid their hands on the animal that was about to be sacrificed. When you feel those hands on your head, remind yourself you're no longer your own man, you're wholly bound to God and his purposes."

Whether those were the exact words or not, they came close. And the thought behind them intruded into

George's consciousness as it never had before. It struck him that the old pastor was addressing even such things as the question of the telephone off the hook.

Margaret was right. Of course Margaret was right. Margaret was always right. Margaret should have been the pastor. She could handle being broken into little pieces and being distributed. She was a marvel and he loved her and he didn't deserve her. That he knew, and he knew nothing else right now.

He was about to drop off when the sound of crying came from Lindley's bedroom.

Margaret was already there when George arrived. She was sitting on the edge of the bed, their daughter gathered into her embrace.

"I thought you were murdered," Lindley sobbed.

There was a rocking movement and a mother's voice, soothing, "It was a nightmare, sweetie pie. There, there—there's nothing to fear—there's nothing to fear—"

Oh, yes there is, George reflected silently as he stood at the door listening. *Oh, yes there is. There's a whole world full of evil out there. It's a nightmare, but it's real.*

He turned and walked back toward the family room, the sound of Margaret's comfort diminishing as he went. "Everything is all right—everything is all right—"

He took to his chair again, turned on the lamp, lifted from the table beside the chair the paperback of *Les Misérables* that Margaret had bought for him. He'd been so blown away by the musical that she thought he might like to read the original book. He'd tried to get into it several times but so far without success. Something always hindered him.

Tonight, once more, he started with the first sentence.

"Clear my mind of everything but this story," he prayed.

The thing that hindered this time was the nagging thought that police didn't really look for criminals anymore. They just wrote down all the information for insurance purposes and so on. Then they waited for the next rape or robbery, at which time they would write down more information. It was exasperating even when you didn't know the victim at all. George could think of any number of unsolved cases in the last year or so. In *Les Misérables*, the policeman Javier sought Jean Valjean tirelessly, tirelessly—and Valjean wasn't even a criminal, not a real one, far from it. Why couldn't there be that kind of dedication nowadays, in real life? It seemed that the only time you could count on good detective work, ever, was in a novel or a film. Think of all the detective novels that people devour. Detective novels didn't leave you with murderers running around loose after all was said and done.

He lay the book aside. This just wasn't the time either. It wasn't the time for *Les Misérables* and it wasn't the time for any detective novel. It was time to erase the day, to erase everything. It was time for sleep—a long, redemptive sleep.

Instead of sleep, a question came.

If he—if he, George McKenna—were a detective on the Rose Templeton case, knowing what he knew at this point, where would he begin?

❀ ❀ ❀

"How is your bug this morning?" Margaret inquired.

"I can tell you this—it hasn't been to sleep."

"I guess not. You didn't take it to bed."

"I didn't want you to catch it."

"That's very thoughtful—of me. Not very thoughtful of yourself." She was making coffee. Suddenly she touched her brow and said, "I can't believe I'm saying this. You don't have a bug and you know it."

"Well, something's wrong, wrong with my body. You should feel how watery my legs feel. And I can't concentrate. I can't seem to process anything."

She had mastered a procedure of filling their cups before the whole pot of coffee was finished. She handed him his, took hers and sat down at the table with the newspaper. It was their rule that whoever went out front for the newspaper got to read it first. This morning the paper could have rotted on the lawn, so far as he cared. As long as the paper was on the lawn and the television screen was blank, there was a kind of hope, wasn't there?

No.

But couldn't it all be a bad dream if the pastor of
Memorial Presbyterian Church prayed very, very hard?

No.

"She made the front page," Margaret said.

"I'm not surprised."

"I don't know," Margaret said. "In this day and time
there are so many murders it takes a special one to make
the front page."

George went on and said it. "This was a special one."

"You know what I think? I think you're suffering from
shock. Shock is a very real thing. I think we should call
Dr. Jones."

George, who had been walking back and forth with
his coffee between the kitchen and the family room,
stopped. He told his wife not to call Seth Jones. "I
don't want to talk to a doctor. I don't want to talk to any
member of our church. Not right now."

"You're hiding!" She had dropped to a whisper, for
Lindley was heard approaching. But the exclamation
point was definitely there and the tone had an edge to it.

They resorted to silence while Lindley ate Cheerios.

"Don't you want some, Daddy?"

"Not this morning, honey."

"Don't you want some, Mother?"

"Not this morning, dear."

When it was time for George to drive his daughter to
school, Margaret spoke up and said she would do it herself.

George said not to bother, he wasn't that sick.

She pointed out that he hadn't shaved, he wasn't dressed, he looked like a bum. She didn't like the idea of her husband, the pastor of Memorial Presbyterian Church, driving up in front of St. Mary's looking like that.

"Besides," she said, "you're supposed to be sick," and she took the Volvo keys from the hook and followed Lindley out the door.

She came back in ten minutes. She said, "Come alive, George. Hell is not upon us. Shave, shower, get dressed, go to work, do *something*."

"I'll tell you what I'm going to do," George announced. "I'm going to find Dusty Case. I can't go back and not preach the sermon that started all of this, but I can, with the help of God, find the man who killed her."

"It must be an offense to our Lord," Margaret said, "when his servants use that kind of language and then attempt to pull his name into it."

"Don't give me any of that holier-than-thou stuff," George said.

And with that, he took the Buick keys from the hook and left, without shaving, without showering, without changing from last night's clothes. The sweater he had on was not enough, but he didn't go back for his coat. You wouldn't have known that spring was on the way. The morning was cold enough to see a wisp of his breath in the air.

Rose Templeton might be dead, but George McKenna wasn't.

CHAPTER 4

The Cooper-Young neighborhood was coming back. The intersection from which the district drew its name sported a storefront gallery, a feminist bookstore, and a place with tables out front. A new restaurant was going in where Young rounded into Cooper, opposite Cafe Olé. But the return of commerce had a precarious air to it because the surrounding blocks didn't seem to know what was going on. Houses remained in disrepair, their faces dull, their settled foundations either choked or naked, with some of the little yards gone to weed and others gone to dirt. There were exceptions of course, splashes of color and other valiant attempts toward revival, but the prevailing mood up and down the streets was languor.

George started out on a street near the fairgrounds.

Although Dusty Case had indicated he had not been back there in years, it occurred to George that the enormity of what he'd done might send him instinctively to something in his childhood for protection. George was no psychiatrist, but he could see this man hiding behind his grandmother's skirts. No way to know if the grandmother was still living, but George figured the impulse might control him whether she was or not. It was worth a try, wasn't it?

The first question he had to settle was, should he knock on doors and pop questions in the manner of Sergeant Friday in the old "Dragnet" shows? Or should he haunt the sidewalks in search of people—old people—who might remember a boy named Dusty? He parked the Buick in front of a vacant lot. Wishing he'd grabbed more than the sweater, he folded his arms and huddled himself the best he could as he paced along. He decided not to knock on doors. After three blocks of finding nobody loose at this hour and season, he changed his mind and picked a shotgun house with a droop to its porch. He knocked on the door and refolded his arms.

The person who came was nobody's grandmother. She was a drowsy-looking female who appeared to be in her middle twenties. A second glance hinted she was still in her teens. She had more mileage than years.

"Isn't this kind of *early?*" she said, inviting George in. She lacked enthusiasm.

George did not enter. Neither did he comment on the invitation. He asked how long she had lived in the neighborhood.

She came to and gave him a piercing look. "What's this all about?" she wanted to know.

"I'm looking for somebody who used to live around here. An old lady who had a grandson named Dusty."

"There's some old lady lives in that house over there." She pointed across the street. "I don't know anything about her except she minds everybody's business."

George was turning to go.

"You sure you don't want to come in and warm up?" she said.

The old lady across the street was waiting for him, it seemed. George could see her standing at the window as he approached. The door opened almost before he could knock. The screen door, however, did not open. A rickety affair, it was still a barrier of sorts.

"Good morning," George said. "I'm hoping to talk with someone who has lived in this neighborhood for a long, long time."

"I've lived here since 1929," she said, "and I can tell you this—back then we didn't have such as goes on over there. Back then it was a decent world. Mulberry Street stayed on Mulberry Street, if you know what I mean. Nowadays, it's everywhere you turn."

He told her he was looking for someone who had a grandson named Dusty. Dusty Case, who would be maybe thirty, maybe forty, maybe older, he wasn't sure.

"I don't recall a boy named Dusty. Why do you ask? Are you with the police?"

"No, ma'am, I'm not," George said. He was on the verge of telling her that he was the pastor of Memorial Presbyterian Church, and then he remembered his rumpled appearance, his unshaven face. He ran his fingers over the stubble on his chin and said, "I'm just a friend who's trying to help."

"A friend of whom? You say you don't even know how old this Dusty is."

George decided to identify himself truthfully, no matter what he looked like. He did so and faced her scrutiny with barely a flinch. He explained that he had not been to bed last night because of the matter that brought him on this search.

Learning that he was a preacher, the old lady opened the screen door and commanded him to come in out of the cold.

He obeyed.

She sat him down in a chair with doilies on the arms. She quickly turned off the soap opera that was on and brushed her hands on her dress as though to wipe them clean. "What kind of help does this boy need?" she asked, starting a pot of coffee.

"The kind that only Jesus can give," he said.

To which she nodded knowingly.

He was glad that she didn't press him about the particulars. He pointed out again that Dusty Case might be older than he. "Perhaps boy is not the right word."

"You're all boys to me," she said, shaking a friendly forefinger. "If my two sons were living, they'd be sixty-three and sixty-five. And they'd still be boys, believe me."

As soon as she had him sipping hot coffee, she picked up the telephone and began to call old-timers in the neighborhood. "Years ago" she had been a member of the Cooper-Young Quilting Club—"back before things changed"—and she set out to call all the ladies who were still living.

While he sat there listening to her ask one after the other if they remembered anybody who had a grandson named Dusty Case, he reflected on whether or not he had been quite truthful in saying that he was someone who wanted to help that person. He was certain that he had spoken the truth when he said that the help this individual needed was the kind that only Jesus could give. But what was *his* role in this hunt? In his very bones he perceived it as chasing the "boy" down and delivering him to the police and to the courts to pay the price for what he had done. At the present, though, he was having to deal with a nagging awareness that his higher responsibility was to find him and offer him the love of Jesus. He rebelled against that brand of grace being expected of him.

During one call, there was a change in the old lady's

voice—"Why, I do remember, now that you mention it! Yes, a towhead, Wilma Smith's little towheaded grandson. Is Wilma still living? *Aw-w-w*, I'm sorry to hear that."

George, who had perked up, deserted hope in an instant. "The grandmother's dead," he said when the old lady hung up. He didn't wait for her to say it.

"Oh ye of little faith," she chided. "Wilma Smith is bedridden now but still with us."

"Where can I find her?" George was standing, ready to leave.

She described the house. She stepped outside and directed him with crisp, youthful movements of her arms. George gathered he was closer to Wilma Smith's address than to where he'd parked, so he left the Buick where it was and proceeded on foot.

The house she described was there, but it was vacant. The windows were bare and George could see into the empty rooms. He knocked anyway, just in case. Nobody came. He went next door and inquired. A young black woman with a brood of three, one on her hip and two at her feet, explained to him that Wilma Smith now lived two doors farther down.

"Sweet Martha Lester took her in," the young woman said.

George, as he walked on, wondered if "Sweet" was part of the name or merely a fitting adjective.

The question hung in the back of his mind when his

knock brought a large, waddly woman to the door. She was the color of coffee with a lot of cream. "Are you Sweet Martha Lester?" he asked.

"I don't know 'bout the 'sweet' part but that's what they call me."

"I'm looking for Wilma Smith."

"Ain't nobody sweet but Jesus," she said quickly, informatively. And then she asked, protectively, why he was looking for Wilma Smith.

George didn't know how to hedge. "I'm hoping she can tell me how to get in touch with her grandson Dusty."

"You know Dusty?"

"—Only through a friend."

They stood at the door, she on the inside, he on the outside.

"Who *is* that, Sweet Martha?" came a woman's frail voice.

"Somebody looking for Dusty. You want to talk to him?"

"If he thinks Dusty's alive, *yes*." The voice had strengthened.

The woman called Sweet Martha cocked her eyes at George.

"Dusty's alive," he said.

She opened the door for him.

A bed took up one end of the living room. Under the circumstances, everything was remarkably neat. The

light of day poured through a window, revealing geome-
tries of color in a quilt that covered Wilma Smith to her
lap. She was wearing a clean-looking flannel gown. Her
head was practically bald, but the gray fuzz appeared to
have been brushed. She was in a crooked position, tilted
to one side, reading a newspaper.

"What's this about Dusty?" she asked George.

George introduced himself. He told the truth about
who he was. He told the truth about why he was looking for her grandson. The anguish from her face almost
undid him, almost stopped him, but he steeled himself
and went on with the whole story. He felt like a surgeon
cutting on someone without anesthetic. He didn't mention Rose Templeton by name, he didn't have to—
Wilma Smith tapped her finger on the open newspaper.

"May I see that?" he asked.

She pushed it toward him.

He had been standing beside the bed. Now he backed
up and sat down in the straight chair that the woman
named Sweet Martha had placed for him. Rose
Templeton's picture looked up at him from the paper.
She was a much younger woman there. He would not
have recognized her at first glance, but he could see her
when he looked. There was more about who she was
than about the murder itself. One year she had
"reigned" as the Queen of Cotton Carnival. At the
moment, George found it hard to care about that. The
last sentence of the piece reported that a suspect, a

vagrant Mrs. Templeton had befriended, was being sought.

George folded the newspaper, leaned forward, and lay it on the quilt. Then he sat there in the straight chair waiting for Wilma Smith to speak. She had not spoken a word since he hit her with the purpose of his call. She had spoken volumes with her eyes but not a word with her mouth. The only mercy he knew how to offer this sufferer was to wait and not press her.

While Wilma Smith had been silent, her benefactress had not. The moan from behind him went on and on, but finally it stopped and the moaner said, "Wilma, you say when and I'll show this man to the door."

No response.

After a while, George asked the bedridden woman if she had any idea where her grandson might hide.

She shook her head. Then, rasping, she spoke. "You've told me your story. Now I'll tell you mine." She swallowed and postponed her story a moment longer. "My daughter's husband was killed in World War II, and the next month she died giving birth to their baby boy. It was up to me to name him, and I named him Dudley Junior after his father. Wasn't anybody to take him but me. What came out when he tried to say Dudley sounded like Dusty, so that's what everybody called him. I had to work, but I had me some good neighbors who helped me raise him. I guess you could say he grew up from pillar to post—"

Her friend had moved to her side and was stroking the gray fuzz on her head. "You don't have to go through with this if you don't want to, Baby Doll," her friend crooned.

"—but I did the best I could. And after I got converted at Billy Graham's meeting at the stadium in '51, I took Dusty with me to the tabernacle—there used to be a tabernacle around the corner—I took him with me every time the door was open and I wasn't working. He memorized so many Bible verses he got to go to camp free in the summer. He was baptized right there in the lake at Bible camp. That's the kind of boy we're talking about."

"Sounds like you did everything you could to start him off on the right track," George said sympathetically.

"He joined the marines when he graduated from high school. That was in the early '60s. I don't have to tell you where he was sent. When he came back from Vietnam, he was somebody I didn't know. He would get some little job and either get fired or leave it. Couldn't hold on to anything. He stayed with me about six months. That was back when I had a place of my own, and I was on my feet. One day he just up and left and I never heard from him again. You know what was strange? You know what hurt? After he came back from Vietnam, he never would let me kiss him."

George was getting groggy. Wilma Smith's story was interesting as well as pertinent, and yet he was beginning to drift, beginning to lose connections. A tambourine hung on the wall nearby and he was not a lover of tambourines. There was a moment when he could not remember exactly why he was visiting this house and who these two women were. He was clear enough to decide that he should call Margaret before long. She needed to know where he was, and on top of that, talking with her would help him to touch base with himself.

Suddenly, Wilma Smith was saying something that captured him. She was explaining that she had been a seamstress in the alterations department of a very nice dress shop on Union Avenue, and that she on several occasions had come into contact with Mrs. Rose Templeton—"a very hard lady to please, always complaining about something. She had enough money to make your life miserable, if you know what I mean. I just can't see her taking in somebody off the streets. Sweet Martha did it for me when I was evicted, but Sweet Martha is a Christian lady." She patted her friend's hand.

"I believe that Rose Templeton was a Christian lady too, Mrs. Smith."

"Well, that could be. I always say, God is just one big surprise after another."

"Tell me," George said, "do you think there's a chance Dusty will seek you out now that he's in this trouble?"

"My heart won't let me believe Dusty did this," she said. "I can't even talk about that part of it."

"But if he did—"

"—I don't think he would give me a thought. I'd like to think he'd run home for me to pray over him, but I don't think he would."

When George asked to use the telephone, he was shown to the kitchen. The telephone hung on the wall beside the refrigerator. A bolt of panic hit him when he realized he was having trouble with the digits of his home telephone number. He finally got it right and then the receiver began to shake in his hand, and he placed it on the hook even as he heard Margaret's "Hello?"

He stood there, waiting to try it again. The impact of his run from his responsibilities was coming down upon him heavily, and he was sure his voice would not work. His legs grew so numb that he sat down at the kitchen table. He leaned forward and lay his head on his arms. It is true, he thought, I am ill.

The next thing he knew, the hand that had stroked the fuzz on Wilma Smith's head was stroking one of his arms. "You've been asleep for 'bout three hours and I thought I better wake you up."

"Yes—uh—I need to pull out of this," George said.

"Let me fix you something to eat. Do you like tuna fish?"

"Thank you, I'm not hungry."

"I think you need some food."

"Thank you, I couldn't eat a bite," George said.

He asked Wilma Smith if she was positive she didn't

have a clue where he might find Dusty.

Wilma Smith closed her eyes and shook her head. It was obvious that she had finished with talking for now.

The woman called Sweet Martha saw him to the door and told him he needed a coat. "I don't know where springtime is," she said.

"I don't either," George said.

"But it's coming," she called as he reached the sidewalk. There was defiant hope in her voice, and it spoke of more than the stalling season.

George still didn't know if "Sweet" was a part of her name or just an adjective. All he knew was that she was an angel.

He got the blocks mixed up. Looking for his Buick was an Easter egg hunt. When he found it, he found that the Easter egg was minus its hubcaps. He walked around it twice, sighing deeply. The hubcaps did not reappear.

He said, "Oh, well." What else was there to say? He could think of some good curses, but he was still the pastor of Memorial Presbyterian Church and he refrained.

He drove from there to the mission downtown on Poplar and asked around. Nobody knew Dusty. Then he went to the soup kitchen at St. Mary's on Third Street. It happened to be noon. Feeling that he looked the part, he actually got in line and accepted the handout of food. He was hungrier than he thought. He inquired if anybody knew Dusty. Everybody was blank. By the time he had made the rounds of all the places that seemed possibilities, the sun was falling.

He drove eastward in a flow of after-work traffic and got as far as his driveway and then turned around, unable to face the George McKenna that awaited him there. That George McKenna and George McKenna the deserter had nothing in common. There was no meeting ground. He headed back downtown, drove across the bridge, took the first turnaround on the other side and drove back to Cooper-Young, back to Sweet Martha's house.

"May I sleep here?" he asked. "The couch would be fine."

"You're welcome to sleep here, but does your wife know where you are? Are you sick or something? If you're sick, you ought to be home where you belong."

"I don't think I'm really sick. I think I'm just mixed up—terribly mixed up. I need some time is what it is."

"And you're a *pastor?*"

"Pastors don't necessarily have it all together."

"That's the truth," she said, allowing an edge of humor.

What was that smell? George was afraid it was cabbage, and cabbage it was. His hostess insisted that he eat. He sat at the kitchen table, trying, while she ate with the invalid in the living room. He could not make himself tell her that he hated cabbage.

Wilma Smith said only one thing to him during the evening, but she said it again and again. "My Dusty's dead. It must be somebody else."

George could understand the sentiment.

The television set was on but George couldn't get interested in anything. He went to the telephone, got his nerve up and called Margaret.

"I won't be home tonight, but I don't want you to worry about me. I'm okay."

"Where are you?" she burst. There seemed more fury than worry.

"I just need some time," he said.

"You're hyperventilating," she said. It was like an accusation.

He didn't know what else to say. He hung up. She was hyperventilating too, he thought.

Sweet Martha had turned the television set off. "We usually have prayer before we call it a day," she told him. "Would you like to lead us?"

"Our God, our help in ages past," George began. He waited for prayer to fill him. Finally he said, "Ladies, I'm confused. I can't pray."

"Say that to Jesus," Sweet Martha instructed.

"Jesus," he said, "I'm confused, and I don't know how to pray."

"Now you're praying," Sweet Martha said.

He was able to get a few sentences out before silence overcame him. Finally, Sweet Martha took over. She was sitting beside him on the couch. She lifted her arms and prayer rolled out of her like a train leaving the station, slowly at first and then gathering speed, reaching a pitch. From the bed, Wilma Smith joined in intermittently and her prayers were like whispers of steam alongside her friend's. Sweet Martha's arms would come down and then, after a while, she would lift them again. She prayed for the whole world before she got around to the situation at hand.

"I pray for Mrs. Templeton's friends and family. I pray for Wilma, and I pray for that boy she raised. You know if he did it or not. We don't know anything, Jesus. We don't know which end is up. I pray for this preacher, and I pray for his wife. I pray for all of us, Jesus. We all need you to reach out and touch us."

George fell to whimpering.

Sweet Martha's arms came down from the air and enfolded him. She began to rock him gently and sing, *"Were you there when they crucified my Lord? Were you there when they crucified my Lord? Oh, oh, sometimes it causes me to tremble—tremble—tremble—"*

❀ ❀ ❀

Except for a few times of wakefulness, George slept for the next two days. It was 4 o'clock in the afternoon when he began to function again. Rose Templeton's funeral was at one, the newspaper said. By now, the mourners would have deserted the grave and he could pay his respects all alone.

Sweet Martha offered him the razor of some man who used to stay there, but George decided the thickening stubble might help him move about unrecognized. The weather had warmed up considerably, and he drove with the windows open. The air was good. He felt that he was coming back to life. It might take awhile to get his balance, but something in the taste of the air told him he was on the way to being himself again. After visiting the grave, he would go home and take a long shower and wash it all away.

He decided to take a left at Yates and enter the cemetery through the side gate. As he was making the turn, he realized that the oncoming traffic was closer than he had judged. In that split second he saw that the closest vehicle, the one with which he was about to collide, appeared to be Harry Beckham's Lexus. He speeded up just in time to avoid contact, but in glancing back to see if it was Beckham behind the wheel, which it wasn't, he lost control of the Buick and hit the stone wall that bounded the cemetery.

There was a clunking sound when he pulled back. The sound continued as he drove on toward the side gate. He drove through and committed himself to the maze of narrow paved lanes that wound through the grounds.

Of the two fresh graves banked with flowers, there was no doubt which was Rose Templeton's. If the abundance of floral sprays was not a strong enough clue, the location was. One of the graves was in a new, flat, barren-looking section. The one that had to be hers was on a gentle slope, where an aristocracy of oaks held a lofty council. George drove back to the gate and parked outside, then walked to the grave. He thought he might want to stay after closing time and the car would signal security. Sitting down under the nearest oak, leaning against its trunk, he gazed at the flowers. Again he tried to pray and could not. He determined to stay there until he could. For the first time in his life, he pondered seriously the matter of a person falling away. His theological training would have him reject the possibility, and yet he had run into cases where a believer did seem to have fallen into the darkness of unbelief.

"I believe in the Father," he said aloud. "I believe in the Son. I believe in the Holy Spirit." He offered the statements in lieu of prayer.

Right now he found more assurance in the serenity of the landscape than he did in his faith. That disturbed him until he reminded himself that God could speak through nature as eloquently as through any other medium.

Shalom, the view seemed to whisper. George was willing to settle for that.

Actually, he had mixed feelings about these cemeteries that pretended to be parks. The flat bronze markers at ground level left the vistas clean, but wasn't there a kind of denial in that cleanness? He remembered the interesting graveyard where he had often ventured as a child in

Alabama. Tombstones of every size. A clutter of marble and concrete angels and crosses and what have you. It was no secret around there that people died.

People died around here too. George had no idea how many members of Memorial Presbyterian he had buried. Enough, he thought. Was it too unreasonable, his sitting this one out?

He found that he could not put Rose Templeton's features together. Trying to visualize her face was like trying to look at the sun. You could look all around it but not at it.

Dusk.

The man who came walking across the grounds had the look of a drifter. He was angling for the new grave. The coat he wore, which was several sizes too large, exaggerated his leanness.

George sat as still as the tree trunk behind him and tried to be a part of it.

At first the stranger was the color of the dusk. George thought he might be black, but then he emerged a white man. He walked around the grave, leaned over and broke off a carnation. He put the carnation to his nose. He sat down on the grass, his back toward George.

"Dusty Case?" George said.

In the next instant, the man was on his feet and running. George, almost by reflex, pushed himself up and was running too. It had been fifteen years since he had tackled a man, but it was time for him to do his stuff again. His lack of helmet and pads concerned him only after he was in the air, diving for the legs. It could have been a good clean tackle if the fugitive had not stumbled on a marker and sprawled. Reality came back in the form of a heel. George felt pain all over, but mostly in his nose. The leg escaped as he instinctively put his hand to his face and touched the sudden blood. He scrambled to his feet and continued the chase.

He was able to grab the coat as its wearer tried to scale the wall. He pulled and the pursued fell backward to the ground, right at his feet. George pounced on him and stilled him. The hold was completely unsophisticated, something left over from his boyhood fights, but it worked.

The smell of alcohol rose to George's nostrils. It told him he couldn't take full credit for the conquest. A streetlight outside the wall came on. Deep stubble blotched the face that looked up at him, and he was reminded that his own face wore a three-day growth. The haze about the eyes made George know just how tired he was himself, made him feel that he was looking into a mirror.

"Dusty?" he said.

A time of waiting and breathing. Then, "My name is Dusty, but I didn't kill that lady."

"Dusty, I'm George McKenna, Mrs. Templeton's pastor."

"I tell you, I didn't kill her."

"Then why did you disappear?"

"Her pastor? *You?*" Disbelief punctuated by a cackle.

"I talked with you over the telephone one day."

"You don't look like a pastor to me."

"Like they say, truth is stranger than fiction."

Dusty struggled to free himself.

George held firm and remained in control. "You say you didn't kill her? How did you know somebody killed her? I don't see you as somebody who reads the morning paper or keeps up with TV news."

Silence.

"And you still haven't answered my question. If you're not guilty, why did you disappear?"

CHAPTER 5

The Buick conked out as they drove into the McDonald's lot. They pushed it into a parking space. It overlapped the lines, but who cared?

"What sounds good, a Big Mac or a Quarter Pounder?" George asked.

"I eat anything," Dusty said.

"Come on, which do you like best? You're bound to have a preference."

"Well, now that you mention it, I guess my favorite's a Quarter Pounder with cheese."

"Sounds good to me too. Coffee?"

"I could use some."

They sat in the back booth, near the restroom door. George faced the rear, hoping to be unnoticed if anybody he knew came in. He reflected on what he had heard so far. Dusty, instead of talking about the death of Rose Templeton, had talked about Vietnam, about the indiscriminate killing, the boredom away from the killing, the escape into drugs, the prostitutes, the prostitutes, the prostitutes.

"Okay," George said, "let's bring it up to date. What about Rose Templeton?"

Dusty told about the Sunday she picked him up at Seessel's and took him home to dinner. The details were much as George had heard them before, but the difference in perspective was interesting. The way Dusty told the story, he had resisted the invitation to spend the night, had gone so far as to tell her he might be just a bum but he knew what was right and what was not. She had made him feel, finally, that he would be doing her a great favor if he would accept the offer. He got the idea, he said, that she, being a widow and all, might be lonely for a man. He had showered a long time and put on her dead husband's pajamas that she had laid out for him. In bed in the guest room he had laid awake in unbelief soaking up the luxury of clean sheets. After a while, he got up and wandered quietly down the hall and found that her bedroom door was open a crack. There it was, spelled out and underlined—*come and get it.*

"Being a preacher, you might not know this, but there's women who like to play games."

"Being a preacher, I know more than I ever wanted to."

CHAPTER FIVE

"I pushed the door open and went in. I could tell by her breathing she was already asleep."

George was afraid he was about to learn something else he never wanted to know. He was relieved when Dusty told him that he began to back away before he reached the bed.

"*Why* did you begin to back away?" he asked.

Dusty didn't have a ready answer. He took the last bite of his Quarter Pounder with cheese.

George waited. "I'd be interested to know," he said.

"—I'm not sure," Dusty said. "One of two reasons, I don't know which. It got to me that maybe the door wasn't locked because—she trusted me. I think that might have had something to do with it. But there was something else too. I wasn't sure I could cut it. What turns me on is something cheap."

They went to the counter for refills of coffee. They still hadn't got to what happened three days ago, but George, without consciously changing his mind, realized by the time they returned to the booth that he no longer believed this man to be guilty of the murder of Rose Templeton.

He said, "I take it you never approached her that way again—never *touched* her."

"There wasn't any sex."

"But there *was* a murder. And you would have to be the prime suspect. You know that, don't you?"

"That's why I disappeared."

"If you didn't do it, who did? Your grandmother and I want to know."

A stunned expression. "How do you know Wilma?"

"Oh, the Lord arranges these things." George couldn't help but smile.

"I don't get it," Dusty said.

"I don't get it either," George said. He was still smiling. They might have been friends, sitting and talking. "I don't get *anything*."

"I wasn't sure she was still alive."

"You should go to see her sometime."

Dusty looked into his coffee and shook his head. "I can't do it," he said, under his breath.

"Why not?"

"It's personal."

"She's an invalid now—did you know that?"

No response.

"She lives with a woman called Sweet Martha. Sweet Martha's what Alabama people used to call a high yellow. She takes care of her."

"Sweet Martha was the first black to move into the neighborhood."

"That so?"

"She got rotten eggs thrown at her."

"Did you throw any?"

"No. I'm a bastard, but not that kind of bastard."

George couldn't pass it by. "Then what kind are you, Dusty?"

"You were asking why I can't go to see Wilma. I'll tell you why, and then you'll know exactly what kind."

George waited.

Dusty mustered his resolve. He proceeded with the background information that Wilma Smith had already supplied. How she had taken him in, an orphan. How she raised him the best she could, how she had taken him to church and seen to it that he learned about Jesus. "Wilma was always good to me. She would've fed me her last bite. 'Hold on to Jesus and live pure,' she said when I went away to Nam. Well. *I didn't hold on to Jesus and I didn't live pure.* You know what? Every time I was with a woman, I could hear her saying that. *Hold on to Jesus and live pure.* Every time I washed up afterward, I could see her hanging her head in shame. I couldn't get away from her. When I came home from Nam and she came toward me with open arms, I felt like there wasn't anything clean about me."

"I've felt that way myself at times," George said.

"I think maybe I could have handled it if she hadn't asked me *did* I hold on to Jesus and live pure."

Being a Presbyterian, George wanted to tell Dusty that if you belonged to Jesus it was Jesus who did the holding on. But he didn't want to negate the requirements of human responsibility. Silent, waiting for Dusty to continue, he went so far as to see the present circumstances as, possibly, a key chapter in the redemption of this man. That was another aspect he would have to be careful with, for what would it make of Rose Templeton's death? A participation in the death of Jesus? Yes, and that was tricky doctrine.

Dusty said nothing more until George asked him how he answered Wilma's question.

"I told her I wasn't going to lie to her, and she knew what I meant by that. She said, 'So that's why you haven't kissed me,' and all of a sudden she looked so old. It was a fact, I had sort of hugged her but I hadn't kissed her. I don't know why I hadn't kissed her, but I hadn't."

"Look," George said, "the kind of bastard you are is the same kind of bastard I am, the kind that all of us are. We've all come short. We've all missed the mark."

"I haven't finished," Dusty said.

"Do."

"—One night—I don't remember how long I'd been home—months, maybe a year—anyway, one night I came home drunk as a coot and fell out on the couch. No way I could've made it to my room and locked the door the way I usually did when I was like that. Wilma was asleep, so there wasn't any scene like sometimes. Next day—it was probably in the afternoon—I know she had tried to get me up to go to work and I hadn't moved a muscle. Anyway, it was later and I was still lying there with my eyes closed and I heard her saying, 'Dusty, Dusty, my love, my heart, my dear little boy'—things like that. Her voice came closer and closer and I still kept my eyes closed and all of a sudden I could smell her breath—her breath always smelled like turnip greens—and she kissed me and I hauled off and pushed her away. I pushed her so hard she fell across the coffee table."

George winced.

"I'm not proud of it, but there it is," Dusty said. "It was bad enough how bent her back was from all those years at the sewing machine, and that wasn't all, she was already twisting up with arthritis all over. 'That Arthur Ritus is the meanest man in town,' she used to say. On top of it all, I haul off and do that. Don't ask me why."

"I don't have to ask you why," George said. "I take it you left soon after."

"I left that same day. I didn't know her back was broken until I heard about it later. I couldn't leave her lying there on the floor, so I picked her up and laid her on the couch. Picking her up probably made it worse."

"Yes, it probably did," George said, for something to say.

"So—now you know," Dusty said.

"What I don't know," George said, "is who killed Mrs. Templeton. Once again, if you didn't do it, who did? Do you have any idea?"

"I have more than an idea."

"I think it behooves you to spill whatever you know."

"I could sure use some bourbon about now."

"Come on, Dusty, you can tell the truth without liquorin' up."

"You sure you don't have some on you I could just wash my mouth out with?"

George almost laughed. "Not quite," he said.

"Maybe just a little to gargle with, to clear my throat?"

A laugh did come. A small one. George couldn't help it. "You don't need it, my friend."

"There's a liquor store down the way. If you've got money in your pocket and want to prove you're a real Christian, I'll lead you to it."

George could see that behind the masquerade of humor was a genuine plea. "I'm afraid you're going to have to settle for a second refill of coffee," he said. The sympathy in his voice was not a complete lie.

George was expecting a name to be offered, or at least a clue to the identity of the murderer, but that was not how it went. Not at first.

Dusty spoke haltingly, looking down. It seemed that he searched for the next sentence, the next phrase, in the depths of his second refill. His intensity grew with each pause. As George listened and waited to listen, there was time to visualize what he was hearing, to watch it as one would watch a scene in a movie.

Rose Templeton was leaving for the golf course. She asked Dusty if he would like to come along. "It's a glorious day and you need some sunshine," she said.

He was about to accept her invitation, then he thought better. "I don't want to embarrass you in front of your friends."

"You said that—I didn't," she said.

"Well, that's how I feel, ma'am."

"Then you must change how you feel. You must begin to see yourself in a new light."

"I'm trying."

"You must see yourself as I see you."

The Jaguar was black and gleaming in the morning sun. Dusty watched it slither down the drive and turn toward Walnut Grove. Then he went back to the television set. "Today" was on. A man in a dark suit was talking about investments. His crisp-looking white collar and his tie, even the angle of the knot in his tie, talked money with as much authority as his words did. Dusty touched the remote and the screen darkened. He got up and went to the mirror in the entrance hall. It was a large mirror. Dusty made it a habit not to look into his eyes when he looked into a mirror. "You must see yourself as I see you," she had said. He stood there and tried, but he could not see himself as Mrs. Templeton saw him.

He went to the cabinet where Mrs. Templeton kept *Wild Turkey*. He had discovered the bottle on a previous investigation. He had not taken one swig then. Now he took the bottle from the shelf and sat down on the floor. After each swig, he smacked his lips and sat the bottle between his legs. He drank until the bottle was empty.

He could barely catch his balance when he stood up. Aiming for the stairway, he floated first in one direction, then in another. As he passed the mirror in the hall, he reached out to the table under it, to steady himself. Everything was blurry. Everything but his image in the mirror. There was no softening of the truth that faced him there. The man was a worm. The man was a blight on society. Dusty placed his hand on a marble bookend. He wanted to pick it up and smash it against the reflection, but that would not do the job that needed to be done.

He made his way to the stairs. Holding to the banister, he made his way up. He entered the first door and was in Mrs. Templeton's bedroom. From the drawer in the bedside table he brought forth, with extreme care, the pistol she had told him she kept for protection. He checked the chamber with the same extreme care. "Yes," he said to himself. He sat down on the side of the bed, the room was whirling.

It was sleep that he wanted. That's what it would be— a long, long sleep.

He lay back on the bedspread and placed the barrel to his temple. He gave himself a moment to reconsider . . . and dropped off. The next thing he knew, Mrs. Templeton was rushing toward him. She was crying out, "No!—No!—No!" She was reaching for the pistol.

Dusty held to it, more by instinct than by decision.

They struggled and the pistol fired.

George left the Buick on the McDonald's lot, and he and Dusty took to the sidewalk. The night was cold and George envied Dusty's overcoat. They walked in silence mostly. The thoroughfare was anything but silent, the traffic whooshing by. Life going on at the usual pace, full speed ahead. George felt oddly separated from those vehicles and the world they represented, though they sliced the air but a few feet away and at any time could swerve and bring death.

He and Dusty turned at the cross street that would take them to George's neighborhood. The traffic thinned to an occasional car. It was strange—the deeper George traveled into residential serenity, the more intense was his feeling of disconnection with the world as he had known it, and especially with the house toward which he was heading. The lighted steeple of Memorial Presbyterian came into view. It seemed impossible that he was the pastor of that church. That church with all its dignity. By the time he and Dusty reached the manse, George was shaking inside and out, and it wasn't all from the cold.

Dusty said, "I don't think I should go in."

"Don't give me that stuff. You're coming in. You're going to sleep here."

They went through the carport. George had the house

key in hand, but the outer door was latched and he couldn't get to the lock.

He knocked.

"Look," Dusty said, "I don't feel right about this."

George said, "This is my house, and I say it's okay."

Margaret came to the door and pulled aside the little curtain at the inset window. Her face disappeared the instant George saw recognition in her eyes. There was a fumbling on the other side and suddenly the door swung open. She unlatched the outer door, and George, pulling it, stood back for Dusty to enter.

It was obvious from Margaret's expression that she had not noticed Dusty when she peeped through the glass. She stood back.

"This is Dusty Case," George said.

"Hello, ma'am," Dusty offered.

"—Hello," Margaret managed to say. She took another step backward.

George wrapped his arms around her. She did not wrap her arms around him.

She said, "I think I deserve some kind of explanation."

George said, "I think you do too."

Dusty was turning to exit through the door he had just entered.

George said, "No, Dusty—you stay."

"I think the elders of the church deserve an explanation," Margaret was saying. "I think the entire congregation deserves an explanation."

George plopped into a chair at the kitchen table. Margaret remained standing, and so did Dusty.

George said he didn't see why the whole congregation should be involved unless somebody had put them onto the fact that he had been out of pocket for two days.

"Out of pocket?" Margaret echoed wryly. "How genteel of you to call it that. *Missing* is what you have been."

"All anyone should have to know," George said, "is that I've been sick. I have been sick. I'm sure that Bill Taylor did an excellent job with the funeral."

"But what was I to tell Dr. Jones when he called to say he had heard you were sick and he wondered if it was that bronchial condition again? I tried to lie for you, but I couldn't. I broke down and cried—yes, I cried—I wept."

"I hope Lindley didn't see you."

"She did. And that's all right. Lindley has to know I'm not made of steel."

"Where is Lindley now?"

"Spending the night with Penny Russell. I decided it was best that she not be around here while you're gone. She needed to get away from—away from your absence."

"Please tell me you hung up before you lost it."

"I didn't."

"How did Doc react?"

"He said 'I'm coming over.' And he did."

George groaned.

Margaret turned to Dusty. "Would you excuse us

please? My husband and I need to discuss some things."

Dusty started for the door, but George took his arm and directed him to the pulled-out chair. Then he followed Margaret to their bedroom and closed the door behind them.

"Is that the man that Rose Templeton took in?"

"—Yes."

"Are you in touch with the police? You *are* turning him over, aren't you?"

"No to both questions."

"In God's name, why not?"

"Do not use his name in vain, Margaret."

"I am not using his name in vain. *In God's name,* why are you not turning this man over to the police?"

"I don't think he's guilty."

"That's not for you to determine. You are not God, you are not the police, you are not a jury."

George told his wife what Dusty had told him, but she would not buy it.

"So Doc paid you a call," he said.

"He did at that. I told him how strange you were acting. You know what he said? He said he thinks you're suffering from depression. He wants to see you. He said there are drugs—"

"That's a very popular word nowadays, isn't it? Depression."

"He thinks yours might have been coming on for a long time, and this—this incident—just triggered it."

George shook his head, slowly. In amusement.

Margaret said, "It's nothing to be ashamed of. A minister is human and just as susceptible as anybody else."

George said, with mock formality, "May I use the bathroom?"

"I suppose so." The bathroom door was behind her. She stepped aside and gestured toward it. "'Tis yours as much as mine."

"Thank you."

When he came out, he found that Margaret had left the bedroom. He returned to the kitchen and she was not there.

"Have you seen my wife?" he asked Dusty.

Dusty nodded toward the den.

She stood at the far end, by the bookcase, telephone in hand, hurriedly winding up a conversation. George entered, but he heard not a word that she spoke into the mouthpiece.

"Who did you call?" he asked.

Was she going to answer the question? Was she thinking up a lie?

"—Dr. Jones." The reply had the ring of truth. "He had told me to let him know when you showed up."

"Don't tell me he's coming over."

"He wasn't there. I just left a message. He'll probably call first."

"Dusty," George said, returning to the kitchen, "let's get our ducks in a row and get out of here. I'm not submitting myself to *treatment*. Do you want to use the bathroom before we go?" George pointed toward the one that was near.

When Dusty closed the bathroom door behind him, Margaret came up to George and took his hands in hers. She looked him straight in the eyes. "You must not go." She spoke in a whisper and yet there was a force beneath her voice. "Please stay and be the man that you are. Be my George."

His arms went around her—tightly. Her warmth was good. "I know this is hard on you too," he said.

"Let's get back to normal," she said. "Let me fix you some supper. I'll even extend the invitation to—him."

"We ate at McDonald's." George was still holding her.

"How about some cake?"

"Great idea," George said, and released her. "Dusty is innocent. I'm sure of it."

Margaret uncovered the cake plate. "I might as well tell you the truth. It was the police I was talking with. I told them he was here. George, we can't hide him. Let them determine whether he's guilty or not."

George stood there trying to control his fury.

From the bathroom came the sound of the toilet flushing.

"Let's get a move on," he said to Dusty when he reappeared. "We're getting out of here."

"I'm not believing this," Margaret said. She sat down and covered her face with her hands. "Dear Lord, is my husband losing his mind?"

"I left the Buick at McDonald's on Poplar," George said, placing the keys on the kitchen counter.

"*Why?*"

He tossed an explanation over his shoulder, told her what mechanic to call, grabbed a jacket from the entrance closet. Returning to the kitchen, he heard Dusty Case say, "Ma'am, I'm sorry about all of this."

George was tempted to take the keys to the Volvo, but he knew he couldn't do that. He was allowing himself a madness he had never dreamed of, but he knew there were limits.

"You'll throw away your pastorate if you keep this up!" Margaret called after him.

He steered Dusty through the carport and toward the gap in the hedge that lined the side street. The beams of the headlights turning into the driveway did not touch them.

CHAPTER 6

A young man in sweat gear was using the automatic teller. His back was to George and Dusty as they approached. George disliked entering the light, but he had checked his wallet and decided that a visit was necessary.

Not until the young man had completed the transaction did George recognize him. Joel Scotney. George greeted him. There was something embarrassing about the situation.

"How's it going, Pastor?"

Joel Scotney's quizzical expression had to be dealt with.

George introduced Dusty. It occurred to him that Dusty didn't look as scruffy as he did himself.

The quizzical expression lingered even after Joel confessed that their arrival had caused him unease. "These are dangerous places," he said. His laughter didn't quite fit. "I make it a point not to come here at night, but here I am, breaking my own rules."

"So you thought we were going to rob you?" George said, trying for humor.

"Or worse," Joel admitted.

"That's how things are today," George said. He started to go on and say, "That's how things have always been," but he caught himself. This wasn't the time or the place to break into a sermon on original sin.

Joel got into his car, sat there a moment, then got out.

George had made the withdrawal and was pocketing his cash when Joel came back and said. "Is something wrong, Pastor?"

George attempted to brush it off casually. "Do I look that scruffy?" he said.

"Of course not. It's just that I—wondered—"

The concern in Joel's voice opened George emotionally and he found that he could not hold back. The recent events poured out of him. No, Joel hadn't heard about George's "disappearance." He hadn't known Rose Templeton. All he knew about her death was what he'd seen on the news. George explained the part he'd played from the beginning and was continuing to play. "Margaret thinks I've lost my mind. Maybe I have, I don't know. What do you think?" The three men stood outside the teller station, still in the bloom of its light.

"Wait a minute," Joel said. He smiled and placed a respectful hand on George's shoulder. "You're the pastor. You're the one who is supposed to have it all together. I'm the one who comes to *you*, remember?"

"God help us all," George said. He looked at Dusty. "Right?"

"Right," Dusty said.

There was only one automobile, Joel Scotney's BMW, parked in the lot. With gesturing hands, he inquired about their transportation.

"That's another part of the story," George said, with a touch of apology. "My Buick's out of commission, and I was planning to call us a taxi. We're headed for Cooper-Young where Dusty's grandmother lives."

Soon, at Joel Scotney's insistence, George and Dusty were passengers in the BMW.

Dusty got sick as they were driving westward on Central Avenue. Joel stopped the car and Dusty got out, but not fast enough. Dusty's overcoat was unbuttoned—it had no buttons—and the front of his shirt and trousers caught as much of the vomit as the curb did.

"Nerves," George said as they drove on. "I can imagine the prodigal threw up a few times on his way back home."

Joel asked Dusty how long it had been since he had seen his grandmother. "Or let's put it this way," he said, "how long has it been since she has seen you?"

Dusty said he couldn't remember. "Let's just say it's

been a long time."

"Then I'm taking you by my apartment so you can clean up." Joel was firm about it. "I have a shirt you can wear, and you might want to shave and shower. This is too big of an occasion for you to go looking like that."

"Or smelling like that," George tossed in. He wished he hadn't, for the intended levity didn't work.

"This whole thing was your idea," Dusty reminded him.

"Listen, I'd be nervous too," George admitted.

"One good slug of bourbon would settle me just right," Dusty said.

"I'm not so sure it would," the pastor said.

Joel Scotney's apartment overlooked Overton Park. Because it was close enough to the zoo to hear the lions roar when his windows were open, Joel had decorated with a tropical theme. A ceramic elephant supported a cocktail tray in front of the white wicker settee. Bamboo poles—they might have been fishing poles, but George surmised they weren't—rose at angles from an urn in one corner. Three large cushions covered with a zebra design were stacked neatly by the window. While Dusty shaved and showered, George and Joel sat on black safari chairs and made small talk.

The small talk came to a point where it had to peter

out or take on substance. George was all for letting it peter out. He was tired and, furthermore, he had disclosed as much of his confusion as he wanted to. But suddenly Joel was drawing him back.

"Do you plan to turn him in?" A nod toward the bathroom.

"I don't know what I plan to do," George said.

"Robert Ashton's a good man to defend him if it comes to that."

"You're right. And that would keep it in the family, so to speak. First things first, though. I want to see Dusty and his grandmother reunited. After that—"

Joel wondered aloud if there was a possibility that Memorial Presbyterian Church might pay for the defense.

"Hey, don't be naive," George said. "In order to secure that, Dusty would have to stand a rougher trial with my elders than the one he would stand in court."

"I bet you can swing it," Joel said, "if you really believe in his innocence."

"I don't know, it's likely that my behavior the last few days has brought my stock down with those guys."

"What's the matter? A pastor has a right to be under the weather now and then, doesn't he?"

"Enough talk about me. How have things been, Joel?"

"You mean—?"

"I mean, how have things been, Joel?"

"—the pastor asked in a kindly tone," Joel said.

"I'm glad the pastor sounds kindly. That is certainly his intention."

"Then I can tell you I'm about where I was when I first came to you for advice."

George didn't have to ask what that meant. It meant that Joel, who said he wanted to be heterosexual, was still fighting balky flames of desire in the other direction and sometimes losing the battle. George had feared from the first that he would not be able to help. He believed that people could change—he certainly believed that the Gospel of Christ could change the heart and give new life—but he had learned that in cases like this the transformation was not as cut-and-dried as some ministers made it sound.

When Dusty came forth clean and shaven and dressed in the clothes that Joel had laid out for him, his appearance tied in with George's thoughts and George said, "Now *there's* a transformation for you."

Joel insisted that Dusty swap his overcoat for one of his that wasn't all that old. Dusty's went into a bag of clothes that Joel was planning to put out for the Goodwill pickup.

"So bond daddies have multiple overcoats," George remarked to Joel. "I'm impressed."

George knocked and waited.

He knocked again.

"Who is it?" The voice of Sweet Martha.

"It's George McKenna. I have a surprise for Wilma."

He motioned to Dusty, who had stalled at the bottom of the porch steps. Dusty took a couple of steps and stalled again.

The door was opening and Sweet Martha was saying, "We were just beginning to pray. Come on in and join us."

When she saw the shadowy figure holding back, she thrust her head into the night.

"Are you who I think you are?" she said.

"Sweet Martha, do you remember me?" Dusty said.

"Lord!" Sweet Martha cried. "Of course I do!"

George, entering, had to get out of the way as the bulk of Sweet Martha barged toward the woman in the bed.

"Wilma child," she said, "your baby's here."

"What baby?" Wilma Smith asked. The lamp beside the bed lighted her blankness.

George, holding the screen door open, reached for Dusty's hand to lead him in. It occurred to him in that moment that he never before had reached out for a man's hand, except in the formality of shaking hands. Occasionally he did find himself in a group where people wanted to hold hands while praying, but he was never much for it, and, if the person on either side of him was a man, he let him do the reaching out.

Suddenly, as Dusty stepped through the door, George realized that Wilma had risen and was on her feet, her bare feet, walking on a rough sea as it were, toward her grandson.

"Look-a-here!" Sweet Martha cried. "You're walking!"

She reached out to steady her friend, but her friend was doing just fine. Sweet Martha began to clap her hands and George joined in. Dusty scooped Wilma up into his arms and received her kiss, and he turned and turned with her cradled in his arms, her gnarled legs protruding from the wadded flannel. His turning became a dance and Sweet Martha took the tambourine down from the wall and began to jangle it.

George, surprised at himself, continued clapping. The slaps of Sweet Martha against the drum of the tambourine achieved a sensuous rhythm and George tried to catch it. He was not entirely successful—he had never had much of a sense of rhythm—but he felt that now he was about to break through to some kind of freedom he had never known before. Vaguely he wondered why he connected rhythm with freedom. But why not? When the sister of Moses led the maidens in that dance of praise after coming safely through the Red Sea, the mood had not been sedate and somber, had it? George could not imagine that it was.

Dusty stood Wilma on her feet, and she caught her

balance and danced back to the bed on her own.

"Are we witnessing a miracle?" George asked.

"I don't know 'bout you," Sweet Martha said, "but I am."

Drunk with it all, George went out to the sidewalk for air. Rose Templeton's death was out there waiting for him in the light rain that had begun to fall. Now that Margaret had called the police, they would be looking for him as well as for Dusty. He tilted his head back and gathered cold, prickly drops on his face.

What was the terminology? Obstruction of justice? Aiding and abetting the escape of a suspect? It didn't make a lot of difference what you called it, George supposed that he would be considered guilty.

CHAPTER 7

The piano recital had already begun when George arrived at the church. A thin but defiant melody tugged him toward the fellowship hall. This was the third year that Miss Olivia Bee had used the facility for her students' big night. Permission the first year had required an act of the church session. Now the function was accepted as custom. George felt almost smug about remembering that tonight was the night, but at the last moment, before pushing the door open, he paused and listened. Was that Lindley's piece? It occurred to him it would be better not to show up at all than to show up late. His unkempt appearance and the fact that he had not entered the church since Rose Templeton's death were strikes enough against him. Those matters, however, would make no difference with Lindley, would they?

Assuring himself that the ascending trills in the air were beyond his daughter's artistry at this time, he pushed the door to enter. He thanked God for the squeakless hinge and for the carpet that muted his footsteps as he tiptoed to the back row of metal chairs and slipped into the empty one on the end, next to Margaret.

Margaret gave him the barest corner-of-the-eye glance. She shifted her weight to the other side of the chair. The move was slight but the message was clear. Don't touch me. An offended woman's classic response.

George had called her every day since the night he delivered Dusty to Wilma Smith. How long had it been? Three nights? Four nights? Margaret had said that the police came only the once. She had told him not to worry, that he would have the privilege of the clergy. Nevertheless, he'd been "laying low" at Sweet Martha's himself, enjoying the spirit and trying to get his mind back together. Margaret had pleaded with him—sometimes gently, sometimes not gently at all—to come home and "be the man that you are."

Well, here he was and this was the reception he got. It didn't wound him, though. He had learned that the don't-touch-me routine was like the first step in a dance.

The piano students sat in a crescent line of metal chairs extending beyond the curved end of the ebony baby grand. Lindley in her green velvet dress sat in the chair next to the one that was empty. She was looking straight ahead, not at George, not at Margaret, not at the performer. She was up next, George gathered, and he could imagine the stage fright. It was perfectly natural, he knew, but he prayed that it would go away, that his little girl would be able to relax and play well.

The young man at the keyboard, all of nine or ten years old and decked out in tie and blue blazer and gray slacks, was Harry Beckham's grandson. George looked for Harry in the audience, and there he sat on the front row. George could read pride in the very set of his shoulders. A confrontation with Harry Beckham—the power elder—George wasn't looking forward to that. His absence would surely come up, and he wasn't sure he was ready to talk about it yet.

Harry Beckham's grandson finished his piece and, with obvious relief, stood up and received applause, to which George contributed automatically. After what passed for a bow, the young man strode to his chair and plopped down.

Something inside of George twisted when he realized that the girl sitting on the other side was rising and heading for the keyboard. The line was peeling off in the wrong direction. Did that mean that Lindley had already performed?

George reached for Margaret's printed program and she relinquished it. He feared the worst—and found it. If the listed order was followed, Lindley McKenna had immediately preceded William Anderson Beckham.

He leaned slightly toward his wife, and she leaned

slightly away from him. He pointed to Lindley's name and asked with his eyes the question to which he already knew the answer. Margaret nodded her head, affirming coldly that he had missed his daughter and her playing of "Country Gardens."

The instant the recital was over, Lindley flew. Even before Miss Olivia Bee had articulated her thanks for the student's hard work and the parents' support.

George found his daughter in an alcove down the hall. She was crying. Not loudly but deeply.

She turned away from him and said, "Mother told me that you probably wouldn't be there."

"She shouldn't have said that." George reached out to her shoulders.

"But she was right, wasn't she?" With that, she turned toward him.

Margaret, who had taken off in the opposite direction, was now approaching from behind. "Darling," she was saying to Lindley, "you played beautifully."

Lindley went into her arms. "No, I didn't. Not really."

"I think you did remarkably well," Margaret said, "under the circumstances." She was looking straight at George.

George turned and walked toward the exit. A few parents dawdled outside the fellowship hall. He paused to chat with them, and to compliment the remaining piano students.

Waiting outside on the steps was Harry Beckham.

"Long time no see," Harry said.

"Oh, come on, Harry. It hasn't been that long. With Bill Taylor in the pulpit, I'll bet you haven't even missed me."

"Bill's been doing a top-notch job. You feeling better?"

"Much better, Harry."

"Good. I've been concerned about you. I might as well confess I've called a special meeting of the session tomorrow night. I realize it's not kosher. You're the one who calls the meetings. But the circumstances are far from ordinary. Do me a favor and make it official. And try to be there yourself if you can."

George, who had asked Joel Scotney to drop him off for the recital, plodded homeward on foot. Margaret and Lindley drove past, and then the Volvo slowed and pulled to the curb. George approached the lowering window, and Margaret asked if he was coming home.

"If I'm welcome," he said.

Margaret didn't say anything, but she sat there as though waiting for him to hop in.

"We're going to the mall for frozen yogurt," Lindley said. It's raspberry day. You love raspberry, Daddy."

George thought he detected forgiveness in her words

and in the sound of her voice. There came a surge of thanksgiving from deep within him, and he almost choked up.

"Thanks, honey, but Daddy's not hungry." George stuck his head through the window and kissed his daughter. "I think I'll just walk on home."

By the time the Volvo drove forward, he had already set his pace. Why was it, he wondered, that the death of Rose Templeton had thrown him for a loop? Was he not ready for a Christianity that cost its participants so much? His theology allowed for it, didn't it? Often he had quoted Dietrich Bonhoeffer's invitation to "come and die." But that was always from a distance. Up close, that brand of Christianity was difficult to deal with. There was no way to get around the fact that he was involved in this recent death. George McKenna had fed Rose Templeton the Word and she had fleshed it out and had lost her life because of it. She had not died for the name of Christ—that, somehow, would have been easier to grasp—she had died, he was beginning to understand, *as* Christ.

So an old woman might rise from her bed of affliction? That was about what it added up to, wasn't it?

Yes.

But still—

The Buick was back in the carport. George wondered what the trouble had been and how much the repair had cost. An arm and a leg probably, like everything else. On top of that, the hubcaps had been replaced. He reached out to touch his automobile, with love, as though to make amends for leaving it in the lot at McDonald's. The proper amends, however, were to be made to Margaret for taking care of the situation—and those were the least of the amends due her.

The Volvo wasn't home yet.

The telephone was ringing when he went into the house. It was his father.

"Where you been, son?"

George wondered how long the phone had been ringing. "Just got in from Lindley's piano recital," he said.

"I mean the last few days. I've called I don't know how many times and you were always out."

"Like I've said before, a man's time isn't his own when he's serving the Lord." He quickly went on to say, "You should have heard your granddaughter. She played beautifully." With the last sentence, he winced inside.

"Why, of course she did. What else did you expect?"

"How have you been, Dad?"

"Not very well."

"Do you get enough exercise, I wonder?"

"Enough to know I'm not a spring chicken anymore."

"Who is?" George said, chuckling.

"When do you plan to come down and see me?"

"It hasn't been all that long, Dad, I was down just a couple of weeks ago, remember?"

Then came the litany of aches and pains. George, as usual, began to feel guilty about he didn't know what. It wasn't his fault that his father was aging and lonely. Blame that on Adam and Eve. He reminded his father once again that he was welcome to come and live with them in Memphis, and his father reminded him once again that he wasn't leaving his abode until the undertaker wheeled him out feet first. The standing refusal of the standing invitation was a source of relief to George, and that was where he met his guilt.

"Don't look for the undertaker too soon," he said lightly. "The Lord isn't ready for you yet." George hated the shallowness of talk like that, but on occasion it worked better than anything else.

After hanging up, George went into the bathroom off the back hall. He lifted the lid and lifted the seat and relieved his bladder. It was good to be in familiar surroundings. It seemed that you were never farther from home than when you were in a strange bathroom. He flushed and stood there waiting to jiggle the handle. He knew this toilet. It would sing and sing until he jiggled the handle. In deference to Margaret's unflagging wishes, he lowered the seat. It was about time, he thought, that he think of her.

She and Lindley entered from the carport as the sound of the flushing died. George, in lieu of something to say, goosed Margaret on her bottom when she passed. She swung around and gave him a quick, scorching look.

Their daughter had caught the action. That was all right with George. He often said he thought the best sex education was for a child to see daddy goose mama on her bottom.

But Margaret said, "Lindley, your father—"

With that unfinished pronouncement, the episode ended. Margaret told him a stack of mail was waiting for him on his desk. Not only the mail delivered at home but a stack that Laura had sent over. "You do remember your secretary—Laura?"

"Cut it, Margaret," George said.

He went to his desk and opened the mail. He felt removed from most of it. He forced himself to read and sort the letters. He was getting back to reality. At least he was trying to.

He devoted himself to the correspondence until Lindley came to the door and offered to play "Country Gardens" just for him.

"A private recital," George said. "I'd be honored."

Lindley still had on her green velvet dress. When George was seated in the living room, Lindley entered from the hall—from the wings as it were. Her fingertips lifted the sides of her dress just slightly as she proceeded to the piano. From her manner, she might have been wearing a floor-length gown and the living room might have been a concert hall. On the bench, before touching the keys, she spread her skirt evenly on each side.

The next moment was electric in its silence, with her hands approaching their placements on the keyboard. George lent himself fully to the occasion. The first notes struck and the melody began freely and with assurance. George had heard it in halting snatches during recent months, but he had never really listened. Now he listened, and it seemed that the lilting notes were sprinkling down on him like drops of a summer shower. His daughter was not only forgiving him, she was cleansing him.

His applause at the end of the piece was joined by Margaret's. She had been standing in the doorway behind him without his knowing it. He looked around at her and smiled, still applauding.

"Not one wrong note," she said.

"Sweetheart," George said to his daughter, "that was beautiful."

Lindley, after taking bows, broke the air of formality and put her arms around him. "I almost flubbed at the same place I flubbed at the recital, but I didn't."

"You know what I think?" George said. "I think you were saving the best for your daddy."

A pleasant mood settled upon the house. It was good to be home. George could almost persuade himself that nothing was different. And yet everything was different, he reflected. At least with him it was. Rose Templeton's death was but a part of it. There was Wilma Smith. You can't see an invalid rise and walk and everything remain the same. His faith had been affirmed, and so had his fear, for miracles were frightening things when they jumped out of the Bible and into your life. He thought about the occasion when Jesus had stilled the stormy waters, and the disciples had been more frightened than before the display of his power.

He told Margaret and Lindley about Wilma, about her rising and walking and what led up to it. He condensed the story, leaving a lot of gaps in it. The point he was trying to make, that God always brought something good out of something bad, lost its focus when Lindley reminded him that the beginning of the story was not the death of Mrs. Templeton but the sermon he preached about the Good Samaritan. "That's where the miracle started," she told him, and he was astonished at her insight. The miracle had begun with the Word. He did not ask, *But where does that leave Mrs. Templeton?* The question did not seem fair at the moment.

In Margaret's eyes he read a skepticism about Wilma's rising and walking—a questioning if not an out and out rejection. She seemed to be asking, *Are we sure this woman was a bona fide invalid to start with?*

Her doubt remained unspoken. George was glad of that, for Lindley's sake. Lindley would have enough doubts of her own when the time came—leave them until then.

After Lindley had gone to bed, he was tempted to take

up the issue with Margaret by quoting something from the Bible. Something like "Oh, ye of little faith." But that wouldn't be fair, because deep down it applied to him as well and he knew it.

"May I join you?" he asked Margaret as she prepared for her shower. George usually showered in the mornings, Margaret in the evenings. He was conscious of the fact that he had not showered in a couple of days, morning or evening, and after all, what better way was there to promote intimacy than to shower together?

"That always strikes me as rather silly," she said, but her eyes let him know the subject was not closed.

"What do you mean, always? We haven't showered together since the first month we were married?"

After a moment, she reached out and touched him.

The redbud trees near the entrance of the church were showing color. Had it come out overnight? Perhaps it had been there yesterday, and George, preoccupied, had missed it. He must come back into focus, he told himself.

Instead of going straight to the office, he went into the sanctuary and stood there inside the door as though to acquaint himself anew with its quiet. He pictured Dusty and Wilma and Sweet Martha sitting down front. He didn't set out to picture them there, but the vision forced itself upon him. The chandeliers were not on and the early sun coming through the windows lighted the threesome dramatically. Wilma stood up and danced. Sweet Martha stood up and lifted her arms toward heaven. Dusty stood also, and clapped his hands.

It was impossible to picture the congregation there, with that going on down front. "Putting on a show" was what the members of Memorial Presbyterian would have called it. Even after the commotion had ended and the participants were once again seated and calm, George still could not visualize the regular congregation present. Many times he had spoken of the members as being a diverse group aptly illustrating the oneness that is in Christ, and now he realized how naive he had been. They were not diverse at all, except as a bank president might not be a doctor, or an engineer an accountant, or an architect a lawyer. Come to think of it, they all looked alike, they all dressed alike. Did some mother-spirit of East Memphis lay out the clothes for the entirety of the congregation each morning? George remembered his first day in Memphis when Harry Beckham drove him around, pointing things out. Oak Hall had been on the tour. "That's where you'll buy your clothes," Harry told him, and the pronouncement sank in. George never wore anything from anywhere but Oak Hall, and so he never felt out of place.

He walked to Rose Templeton's pew and sat down. He did not sit by the aisle—that was her spot—he sat next to her spot.

Mrs. Templeton, what do you think about all of this?
I think it's about time you call me Rose.
Rose—
He caught her voice and then he lost it.

Aloud, he quoted her from memory: "I doubt that the Gospel has ever been *safe*."

He did his best to shrug it all off before he entered the office area.

His secretary returned his greeting and said she hoped he was feeling better.

"Much better, thank you," George said. He was glad that Laura was strictly business and not full of questions.

After discussing odds and ends that had come up during his absence, he went into his private office and closed the door. A list of broken appointments, in Laura's neat handwriting, topped his desk. Attached was her note asking when to reschedule. The list was not as long as George expected.

Using the intercom, he asked Laura about the others.

She explained that she had referred some to Bill Taylor, the ones that seemed suitable for him, and he had taken care of them. "I trust that was all right," she said.

"You're a gem, Laura." George asked her to get in touch with those individuals who had been canceled and set them up at their convenience. He didn't have to say "any day except Friday." Laura knew that he liked to keep that day as a cushion in case the Sunday sermon wasn't complete by then.

Through the window, he saw Bill Taylor drive up. He went out to the corridor to pat him on the back.

"I hope you're feeling better," Bill said.

"Much better, thank you. I hear that you've been doing a top-notch job."

They walked toward Bill's office.

"My sermon on Sunday wasn't all it should have been."

"What was your text?"

"Isaiah in the temple. 'I saw the Lord high and lifted up.' It's one of my favorite passages."

"One of mine too," George said. "My friend, there's no way that a sermon on Isaiah 6 could measure up to its potential. It's packed. What was your final emphasis?"

"This question: Where was Isaiah when he saw the Lord high and lifted up?"

The two men delivered the answer in unison, nodding at each other. "In the temple."

That lofty vision was necessary for true worship, George knew, and yet he was learning to appreciate, as never before, the God who had descended to the lower levels for the redemption of his people. Who still descends, George was learning. Who still reaches out and touches whom he chooses.

George resisted the temptation to accompany Bill into his office and tell him the story of Wilma's miracle. He imagined the polite unbelief and went no farther than the door.

"By the way," he said, "thanks especially for taking Mrs. Templeton's funeral. I sort of let you down on that one."

"Don't mention it," Bill Taylor said.

On the way back to his own office, George decided to prepare for Sunday morning a sermon on one of the scenes of healing in the New Testament. He couldn't stand up there behind the pulpit in Memorial Presbyterian Church and tell about Wilma. It just wasn't Presbyterian doctrine. He would stick to a biblical account.

He spent most of the day trying to decide which biblical healing to use. None of them seemed to quite fit. Toward the last he folded his arms on his desk and cradled his head and prayed for guidance. It was then that he realized what he had been doing. He had been trying to select a text to fit what he had to say, rather than the other way around. Not only was he going about it all wrong, he wasn't really sure what he wanted to say.

Laura on the intercom: "Mr. Harry Beckham has called to remind you of the meeting tonight. He hopes you can make it."

George looked at the intercom speaker. He determined to arrive at the meeting before Harry Beckham did.

For supper, Margaret served a concoction of tamales, chili, chips, and cheese. It was a favorite of George's, but on this occasion he ate only one helping.

Margaret said, "It isn't as good as usual, is it?"

"I think it's excellent. It's just this meeting. I want to be there before Harry."

"Is he up to something?"

That was his Margaret. She was herself again. She *was* with him.

He said, "Oh, I don't think he's up to anything, but I want to hear the first of it if he is."

When he drove into the church parking lot and saw the gathering of cars, he figured that the meeting had been called for seven instead of seven-thirty, the usual time for meetings of the session. He couldn't help but wonder if it was on purpose that he was not informed.

Every head turned toward him as he entered the room. He received a buzz of greetings. As soon as the meeting was called to order officially, Harry Beckham proceeded with what they had been discussing.

"Pastor, first off, we want you to know how much we appreciate your ministry here at Memorial Presbyterian. You've been a blessing to this church in the past, and I'm confident you're going to be a blessing to this church in the future. As for the present, however, we're offering you a three-month leave of absence. With pay, of course."

"I don't understand," George said, skittering a glance at the others present.

"Dr. Jones tells us that you're having a breakdown of some kind."

"Dr. Jones has not examined me."

Harry Beckham retorted, "Dr. Jones has not examined you because you have been out of pocket."

"Am I to account for my whereabouts every minute of every day?"

"We realize that a man with your responsibilities is under all kinds of pressure, and we think a long rest is in order."

"This is—extreme."

"I wish someone would offer me a three-month leave of absence with pay." There was a ripple of genial agreement throughout the group.

"And who would preach while I'm out of the pulpit?"

"Bill Taylor does a fine job," Harry Beckham said. "If after three months you feel you've got your head together, we'll start afresh."

"My head is together right now," George said. "But— I will—prayerfully—consider your offer."

CHAPTER 8

The next day he received a telephone call from Sweet Martha. She said she thought he'd want to know that the police had picked Dusty up. He'd been charged with murder in the first degree and was being held without bail.

George moaned.

Sweet Martha said, "I told Wilma not to worry, we knew somebody who could get him a good attorney."

"Dusty's not guilty, you know."

"Guilty or not, that boy's going to need a lawyer."

"I know someone who just might take this on," he told her.

"The problem is, we don't have any money."

"I understand that."

"Bless God," Sweet Martha said.

"You might want to wait on that," George threw in. "I can't promise anything."

"Oh, I never wait to bless God. I always bless him first. Then I just stand back and watch him do his stuff."

"How is Wilma taking it?"

Even as George asked the question, he had a flash of Wilma backing toward the bed and lying down as though in a film reversed. So it was not a surprise when Sweet Martha reported her friend to be laid up again. The surprise was that Wilma's decline had preceded Dusty's arrest and was not a result of it.

"That's how it is with miracles," Sweet Martha told him. "Sometimes they last and sometimes they don't. You just have to enjoy 'em what time there is. It's better to be well for three days than not to be well at all."

"I guess so," George said, and he marveled at her maturity.

❀ ❀ ❀

"Say where," George said, shouldering the telephone against his ear while he doodled on a scratch pad.

"Lulu Grille?" Robert Ashton submitted.

George suggested that they try somewhere else this time.

"Hungry for barbeque?" the attorney inquired.

"Always hungry for barbeque," George said, and punctuated his words with an exclamation point on the scratch pad.

CHAPTER EIGHT

They met at Brad's—Robert Ashton's choice—a small and unpretentious storefront restaurant across the street from Summer Center. The tables were not spotless and neither was the floor. Here and there the vinyl seats of the booths were wearing through. Still, to anyone who liked pit barbeque, the atmosphere was inviting. The sound of the chopping, the aroma of the cleavered pig meat, the sloshing of the hot sauce. One took these in and gathered that Brad knew what he was about and what he was about was good Memphis barbeque, not packaging.

"I thought I knew all the good barbeque places," George said. "How come I never heard about this one?"

"Well, preacher, it's like this: those of us who frequent Brad's try to keep it a secret for the most part. Who wants to get run over by the crowd?"

They received their paper-wrapped sandwiches over the counter and took them to a booth that had been vacated but a moment before. Robert Ashton pulled a paper napkin from the holder and ran it about the surface of the table.

"Last time we lunched together," he said, "was the day Rose Templeton was murdered. Do you think they're close to solving that yet?"

"Interesting that you bring it up." George bit through the thickness of the sandwich, chewed, and made a sound of pleasure to let Robert Ashton know what he thought of the taste.

Between bites, he related Dusty Case's story and his need of defense.

A smile came to Robert Ashton's face and George was confused until he heard, "I thought we were going to pick up where we left off—on the Resurrection."

George wanted to say that this whole thing was directly connected with the Resurrection. But that would have been impossible to prove. Just as the empty tomb itself was impossible to prove.

He said, "Here's an angle for you. I believe—as surely as I believe that Jesus came out of the grave—that this man is innocent of Mrs. Templeton's murder."

"As I said before, I don't necessarily have to believe in someone's innocence in order to represent them."

"I understand. But you're bound to care—personally."

Robert Ashton granted that this was true. Then he said yes, he would take the case.

George expressed relief.

"Under one condition," Robert Ashton added. "That I charge only a token fee."

George instinctively ducked his head—whether to give thanks to God or out of embarrassment, he could not have said. The embarrassment, if that was what it was, came from his observation that many clergymen, because of their office, expected something for nothing.

He looked up and said, "No—let the fee be on me."

"You're the boss," Robert Ashton said, crumpling the

empty sandwich wrapper into a ball.

George had one more bite. When it was gone, he crumpled his wrapper and then shook Robert Ashton's hand.

"You know what I think?" George said. "I think you must be a Christian whether you know it or not."

Before leaving, they went back to the counter and each took a toothpick from the glass jigger. They stood on the sidewalk winding up their conversation and picking bits of pork from their teeth—unashamedly redneck style—the pastor of Memorial Presbyterian Church and one of the city's up-and-coming lawyers.

🐚 🐚 🐚

George's visit with Dusty was almost over when Dusty said, "By the time they get through with you, you're not sure of anything."

The guard, a black female whose muscled presence decreased the area, stood nearby.

George said, "You haven't confessed, I hope."

"No—I don't think I have."

"Don't *think* you did? "George's voice was down to a whisper, but his emotion stormed through. He glanced around. "Listen to me, Dusty Case. Stick to your story and don't confess. Not unless Robert Ashton advises you to. He's your counsel."

George couldn't believe that he was telling this man

not to confess. He, a pastor whose theological system demanded that sin be confessed. Was it permissible to consider first, in cases like this, the wiles of the judicial system?

He leaned closer to Dusty. "Your story sounded quite believable to me. I feel very strongly that it *did* happen that way."

Dusty looked distracted, and then he zeroed in on something. He said, "The overcoat. Take it back to your friend."

"I'm certain that Joel Scotney would want you to keep it."

"I got no use for it here. Please take it back and tell him thank you."

"All right."

"Ask 'em for it. I think they'll give it to you."

"Yes, I think they will."

"Tell 'em you're my preacher."

"I'm leaving a Bible for you. It's an easy translation. Read it every day."

The guard looked at her watch.

"If I'm your preacher," George said, "let's have a word of prayer before I go."

Quietly, he prayed for the man across from him, prayed for truth, prayed for mercy, prayed for Wilma Smith, prayed for himself. When Dusty began to speak after the amen, George interrupted with a postscript. "Thank you, Lord, for providing Robert Ashton."

"Preacher," Dusty was saying, "you don't happen to have a little whiskey on you, do you?"

"You know I don't have any whiskey on me," George said.

"If you could get ahold of some, just a little, and slip it to me. Just enough to wash my mouth out would help."

The guard stifled a smile efficiently. With a motion of her hand, she signaled the end of the visit.

Margaret met him at the door. Something had happened, something was wrong. It was in her eyes.

"What's the matter?" George asked.

She kissed him soberly and said, "It's your father."

"Heart attack?"

She nodded and he could tell there was more.

"Is he dead?" he asked.

"He's with the Lord," she said.

The first thing he did when he reached the house in Florence was to pick up the telephone and call Harry Beckham in Memphis.

"Harry, I've decided to take the three months," he said, having settled his mind about this on the drive down.

"So sorry to hear about your father," Harry said, "but I guess it was God's time."

"Yes. Uh—thank you, Harry.

"How are *you*, George?"

"Not quite ready to say, 'Blessed be the name of the Lord,' but I'll get there."

"Was it sudden?"

"Not really."

"How old was he?"

The question came close to amusing George. He had a theory that when a man inquired about the age of a recently deceased acquaintance he quickly referred to a mental timetable comparing that age to his own. He toyed momentarily with the idea of asking Harry how old *he* was. He couldn't do that. He told him that his father would have been seventy his next birthday. He figured that Harry, for all of his physicality and keeping in shape, was in his late sixties.

"He didn't leave a lot of unfinished business," George said, "but there's the house to deal with, and other details, and there's only me. Having the time off will certainly simplify matters."

"Well then, 'all things work together for good,' don't they?" Harry's voice, when quoting from the Bible, took on a different sound.

George, hoping his didn't, supplied the rest of the verse: "'to them that love God, to them who are the called according to his purpose.'"

"It's understood, Pastor, that you qualify in those regards—and I don't doubt that Bill Taylor does too. Yes, sir, you get yourself back to normal and don't worry a minute about your responsibilities here. Bill Taylor does a bang-up job."

George lay awake in his old room, in his own bed. Margaret and Lindley would be driving down early tomorrow. The funeral was scheduled for 11 o'clock. George had considered spending tonight in a motel, but that seemed a waste of money.

This was the first night he had gone to bed in his old room since he married. It was so easy to make the trip from Memphis to Florence and back in a single day. Now he thought about all the times his parents had asked him to stay over. He knew that feelings of guilt were inevitable when a parent died. He had counseled a number of persons to be prepared for those feelings and not to let them take the upper hand. He was not surprised then to find himself lying there regretting that in all these years he had not stayed for a longer visit. Even when his mother died, he and Margaret and Lindley, the baby Lindley, had stayed at the Holiday Inn. It had been more convenient.

Now it occurred to him that the bed sheets might not have been changed since his mother's death. Compared to the sheets that he remembered smelling of sun and wind, these did exude a mustiness. Here he lay, it seemed, in the past. Here he lay where for a time when he was quite young he had believed that a snake lived under the bed. Where for the years under this roof he had taken his hurts and disappointments. Where on numerous occasions he had wrestled with himself about what his father called "purity"—sometimes winning, sometimes losing. This was also the retreat where, when the time came, he had wrestled with God about his call to ministry.

Wrestled? Yes, he still thought that was the right word for the fight he put up. What he wasn't sure of was the term "call." What was a call to ministry other than a finding of oneself corralled with only one passable gate ahead? George remembered the words of the old preacher who had delivered his ordination sermon: ". . . You're about to get the hands laid on you. Do you know where that started? . . . Back in the Old Testament when they laid their hands on the animal that was about to be sacrificed. When you feel those hands on your head . . . you're no longer your own man, you're wholly bound to God and his purposes." George imagined that most of those creatures about to be sacrificed had sensed what they faced. He imagined—no, he knew—that they too had struggled against it with all their might.

Perhaps he should have fought harder. Surely the individual who was fit for the ministry would not have gone haywire over the death of Rose Templeton, would not have involved himself with the prime suspect, would never have allowed Sweet Martha to cuddle him against her cordial breastworks.

I never claimed to be the right material, he reminded God. I never pretended to have what it takes.

He turned back the covers, got up and went to the bathroom. He decided to stay up and wait for sleepiness. The chill of the house called for more than the Jockey shorts he was wearing. He had not put his robe in the bag. He padded for the door of his father's bedroom, and quietly, as quietly as if his father were alive and sleeping there, he entered and searched in the dark for the robe he had given his father years ago, the one his father still wore—or had worn until now. It hung over the post at the foot of the bed. George put it on and began to pull at the disarray of bedcovers, to at least straighten them, and then, with the smell of his father rising to his nostrils, he went on to make up the bed the best he could. This was not his "area of expertise." His father's slippers were on the floor beside the bed. Wearing the robe and the pair of slippers, he made his way toward the living room.

The smell of his father—it was not unpleasant—went with him and remained with him as he settled down in his father's comfortable chair. He switched on the table-lamp and picked up the Bible that always lay there. He turned to Psalm 90 and began to read. He knew the psalm by heart, but somehow it was always reassuring to see the Word of God in black and white. *Lord, you have been our dwelling place throughout all generations.* The worn leather of the binding and the well-thumbed pages were also redolent of his father. The chair, the robe, the slippers, the Bible, all evoked the man from whom he had sprung. It was as though George once again sat in his lap listening to him read Scripture. That was how it had been almost every night of his childhood. The printed words of Psalm 90 had blurred by the time he reached the last verse. *May the favor of the Lord our God rest upon us.*

George remembered the hardware store, its subtle aromas—nails, chain, sandpaper. Blend them with Lifebuoy soap and Old Spice shaving lotion and throw in some pipe tobacco and you got a whiff of his father. He remembered liking the scent and the feeling of well-being that came when it surrounded him. "Well-being" was of course not a child's term, but that was how George thought of it now. Perhaps a "feeling of belonging" best described his identification in his father's embrace, in his father's world.

Suddenly the loss, which until this moment had withheld its impact, came down upon George and choked the air from his lungs.

His father's minister was new in Florence. George had

known him in seminary, but not well. George appointed the entire service—Scripture, hymns, and all—to him. Having done that, it was hardly fair for George to wince when the organ began the strains of "In the Sweet By and By" as the closing music. He liked hymns about the majesty of God and the glory of his purposes. Hymns packed with human sentimentality were not for him. But the truth was, his father had loved "In the Sweet By and By." It was one of the regulars he had whistled around the house. Margaret reminded George of that when she heard his whispered "Oh, no."

"In my opinion," she said in the funeral home limousine on the way to the cemetery, "it was exactly the right touch. I guess I shouldn't put it that way. I make it sound superficial. But you know what I mean. It was fitting. And if you really believe what you claim to believe—if you really believe what you preach—you *shall* 'meet on that beautiful shore.'"

The procession was passing the hardware store. The present owner, out of respect for the previous owner, had closed for the day. In all probability he and his family rode in one of the automobiles that followed. A wreath of red carnations hung on the door of the hardware store.

"I did think the minister's remarks were excellent," George said.

"Couldn't have done better yourself, huh?" Margaret nudged his shoulder with hers.

"Oh, I don't know about that," George said, and looked at her and smiled.

The ride was smooth. The interior of the limousine was quiet, insulated from the world.

George backtracked. "What do you mean, if I believe what I preach? Shouldn't it be, if we believe what we believe? You do believe too, don't you?"

"Yes," Margaret said. But then she added softly, "Most of the time."

You could trust Margaret to give an honest answer.

"I feel like we're floating," Lindley said.

❀ ❀ ❀

They sat in the folding chairs facing the casket. The canopy above them palpitated in the breeze. It was a beautiful day for a funeral, if funerals had to be. Sunlight splashed on the flowers beyond the line of shade.

"I am the resurrection and the life . . . " The words were so familiar that George was dulled to them. He tried to take them in as new and startling, and could not. Usually, of course, in these circumstances he was the speaker and not the receiver. It was one thing to spout them and another to absorb them. He wished that he could hear those words with the wonder the first hearers must have experienced. They were either the most profound words ever spoken, or they were pure tommyrot.

Thoughts of Rose Templeton and her death horned in

on George's consciousness. He resented the intrusion a little, for it seemed unfair to his father right then. She had her send-off, this was his. But there was the rub— George had not been present at hers. *In the sweet by and by we shall meet on that beautiful shore.* He tried to apply that hymn to Rose Templeton as well as his father. Their deaths, when you came to think of it, resulted from bites of the same historic apple. Historic? Yes, George affirmed once again. But he quickly revised the text of his musing—bites of the same historic piece of fruit. The Book of Genesis did not identify the variety. It only mentioned the fruit's beauty and desirability, and its deadliness. George had noticed that most of the people who said "apple" were those who took the story lightly. It disturbed him to think that he would pick up their vocabulary.

As the minister delivered the final prayer, George's mind went its own way—from the Garden of Eden to an old swimming hole right there in north Alabama. His father, who swam there as a boy, had talked of it and talked of it, and once had taken him there to see it. But the venture had not been as simple as it sounded. They had hunted for the place one whole afternoon. George had begun to feel sorry for his father because he couldn't find his old memory. And then, by golly, hidden by a band of willows, there it was, in hallowed privacy. His father in pure celebration had stripped to nothing, had stood on the large outcrop of rock that served as a diving perch, and had invited him to shuck his clothes also. George, maintaining the sanity of his twenty-five or twenty-six years, had warned of debris beneath the surface of the pool, had warned of snakes, and who knew what. He had not removed a stitch himself. In that moment before his father dived, George took in against his will the beginnings of death in his father's white and pink naked body—the deepening folds, the downward nipples, the gray below his pot. The mercy of God had brought his father safe and exhilarated from the pool, but the prophecy written upon his nakedness had now been fulfilled.

The gathering was breaking up. George and Margaret thanked the minister. So did Lindley, extending her hand as her parents had done. Out from under the canopy, George returned to the present and chatted with lingering friends. He was surprised to see Joel Scotney, who stood off to the side, separate.

"I didn't know you were here," George said, approaching him.

"It was the least I could do," Joel said.

"Why don't you come over to my father's house and help eat the food his neighbors brought over?"

"Yes, do," Margaret said. She told Joel that she and Lindley were heading straight back to Memphis for a birthday party, and it would be a shame if all of the food at his father's house went to waste.

Over a whopping slice of coconut cake, Joel asked about Dusty Case.

George brought him up to date.

Then there was no more conversation about Dusty.

"Are you staying here overnight?" Joel inquired.

"Afraid so. Tomorrow I put the house on the market."

"Were you an only child?" Joel asked.

"I had an older brother," George said. "He died of leukemia when I was quite young."

"We have much in common. I had an older brother. He was killed before I was born. He was five, I think."

"How was he killed?" George inquired.

"Hit by a car. He was in my father's care at the time. My mother never forgave my father, and he left her when I was less than a year old. I hear he drank himself to death."

"You never saw him as you were growing up?"

"Never saw him at all that I remember," Joel said. "Never saw a lot of my mother either, for that matter. I was given to my aunt to raise. Maybe that was best. My mother held a steady job in a department store, but she was straight out of Tennessee Williams. Always talking about the handsome young men she dated when she was a girl in Clarksdale. Always lamenting the choice she made. She would say things like 'Where did all the cotillions go?' right up to the day she died."

It seemed to George that Joel had more in common with Dusty Case than with him. Both had grown up fatherless. One raised by a grandmother, one raised by an aunt. But what a difference between the grandmother and the aunt. George doubted that Wilma Smith's world had ever included the word *cotillion*.

As he and Joel chatted on casually, George's mind took a side trip—the fatherless aspect. That condition, he understood, could lead to homosexual tendencies if other contributing factors were aligned. Evidently some of those other factors were aligned in Joel's case and not in Dusty's. It was all such a mystery to George, and he acknowledged it as such.

"I hate to eat and run," Joel said, "but I have three hours ahead of me."

"Hang around and spend the night. I'll wake you up early—four, five, whatever—you can be back by nine."

Joel appeared to consider the proposition seriously. Then he said, "No, I don't think I should."

"I could use the company."

"I appreciate the invitation," Joel said, "but I'd better not."

Still, he didn't rise.

"More cake?" George asked.

"No, thank you. That was quite good, though."

"More anything?" George swept his arm toward the buffet in the dining room.

"No, no—I've had plenty, thank you." Joel placed the

fork and the empty plate on the coffee table and continued to sit in the rocker that George associated with his mother. "Were you close to your father?" he asked George.

"Yes and no," George said. "You know how it is."

An awkward lapse. George wished he hadn't put it that way.

"No. I don't know how it is," Joel said.

"Yes—well—" George let the subject go. "It was really great of you to come down for the funeral. It means a lot to me."

He sat slightly forward, ready to rise when Joel did.

Joel commented on the collection of candlesticks on the mantel.

"My mother's," George said.

"They're lovely," Joel said, and the rockers beneath him began a lazy to-and-fro.

"She was always on the hunt for pretty candlesticks."

"Did your father have a hobby?"

George settled back into his father's chair and contemplated. "Hmmm. He enjoyed reading his Bible. I guess that could classify as a hobby. And he loved baseball. Played on any team that would take him. Catcher. He was a good catcher." Suddenly George remembered something. "I'll bet his mitt is still under this chair," he said. He leaned over and brought it forth from behind the floor length slipcover. He slid his hand into it and lifted the worn and scuffed leather to his nostrils. He breathed in. How could he have forgotten this smell when he was identifying his father's remaining aura last night?

Joel reached out for the mitt and George relinquished it.

Joel duplicated the ritual of smelling the leather. "I was a nerd," he said. "Didn't play any sports. Wasn't good at them."

"I played a little football. That's not to say I was any good at it. One of the differences I had with my dad was that he liked baseball and I liked football. I guess you could say that neither of us had much respect for the other's sport."

Joel lay the mitt aside. He laced his fingers behind his head, looked upward, continued the slow rocking. "The first male that I was ever attracted to was the star quarterback at high school. He was everything I wasn't. I can see from here what a cliché he was, but at that time he was everything I wanted to be."

Was Joel opening up to another talk about his struggles? Hearing of the quarterback idol, George experienced an empathy with Joel that he had never felt before. He could see how that kind of admiration, that of the unglorious for the glorious, with particular circumstances, might trip into something else, something much more complicated. He knew from previous sessions with Joel that there had been a string of such idols since high school, and that several of them had involved the actual man-to-man worship that he and Joel both believed to be out of sync with God's Holy Word. He knew too that presently this young man had a certain straight friend in focus and was fighting his desire to approach him.

George took this opportunity to come right out and ask if he was winning the fight.

Joel said "I—" The pronoun dangled for a moment. "I find that it doesn't do much good to talk about it. And I need to hit the road anyhow." He was rising from the rocker.

George, accompanying him to the door, said, "I'm available whenever. You know that." He went on to tell Joel that officially he was taking three months off, but not to hesitate to get in touch at any time.

George stood on the porch as Joel drove away. He then went inside and began going through his father's effects, deliberating what there was to be done.

Time passed.

A knock at the door.

On the way to answer it, George looked out the window and saw that Joel's BMW had returned to the driveway. He quickly glanced around the room. Had something been left? Not that he could tell.

He opened the door.

"Long time no see," George said, smiling.

"I've decided I do want to talk after all," Joel said. "There's something I think I should tell you."

CHAPTER 9

The strange thing was that it seemed so natural. No conscious decision had preceded the embrace. George had opened his arms to receive the broken young man as he might have received a son. Or a father. He stood there holding him, remembering that his father at some point had replaced hugs with punches. Now George realized for the first time what a poor substitute the macho ritual was.

"Have you not suspected it was you all along?" Joel said.

"It never entered my mind," George answered.

After easing apart, George placed one arm around Joel's shoulder in the more accepted manner and walked with him to the couch.

The counseling sessions must come to a stop. If Joel still wanted help, he would have to seek it elsewhere. George didn't claim to be an authority on the subject anyway. He sat down on the couch beside Joel. Looking across at his father's chair, remembering the arms he had known as a boy, he hooked Joel's neck and drew him close.

They remained locked and George began to wonder if this kind of contact might fulfill some need, some perfectly innocent desire, some God-intended hunger for communion with one's own sex. Might that be how one's own sexual identity was established? Could it be that deprivation of this intensified and distorted the urge until it led to erotic confusion?

If so, wasn't it possible that the clench he had on Joel might be of therapeutic value? Perhaps his counseling sessions with Joel should continue after all, but change in character.

He was conscious of the fact that he had said almost nothing since Joel's declaration. What was there to say? How dare you like me? The truth was, and George admitted it to himself, that the ego fed greedily on any compliment, out of order or not.

Joel fell asleep with his head against George's shoulder.

It was almost dawn when George woke up, still there on the couch.

Joel Scotney was gone.

George stayed in Florence two more days, doing things that had to be done.

It was raining the afternoon he set out for Memphis. It was raining when he crossed the bridge to Sheffield, raining when he stopped for gas on the outskirts of Corinth. He used the restroom and was saddened by the penciled message on the wall above the urinal: *I was here at 3:15. Where were you?* Then it was back to the darkening rain and the whipping of the windshield wipers.

The closer he got to Memphis, the more he questioned his handling of the Joel Scotney situation the night after the funeral. But he kept telling himself that the practice just might help in cases like Joel's, where the individual was not happy with his impulses. He doubted that it would change anything for those who were content with homosexuality. If one had chosen that life as one's own, it was between that individual and the Creator. George was not one to pontificate except to point people to Golgotha where God's judgment and God's mercy came together. His main thought about homosexuals was that "gay" was something of a misnomer. Of the homosexuals George had known, it seemed that all wore a desperate lightheartedness over a burden of insatiable longings. The real desire, one had confessed to him, was to have sex with a truly masculine man. And the minute the lust was consummated, one had to face the emptiness of the triumph, the realization that the lover was not truly masculine after all. *I was here at 3:15. Where were you?* The cry of lostness. How shocked the lost would be to find it was union with Jesus they were seeking all along. *I was on the cross at 3:15*, the Word could answer. *Where were you?*

George decided that his embracing of Joel amounted to the same kind of charity that Rose Templeton had extended to Dusty Case. No, on second thought he didn't like the sound of that—the pride. It was for God to know what was charity and what wasn't. But the connection was there. George didn't know quite why, but he seriously doubted that he would have taken Joel into his arms if Rose Templeton had not taken Dusty Case into her house.

Ahead, on the shoulder of the road, an unlighted car materialized in the rain. Noticing the two figures standing beside it, George slowed, but when they began to wave him down he instinctively kept to the road and increased his speed. The images of the two stayed with him. They appeared to be male and female. They appeared to be young but as scruffy as the old Ford behind them.

He felt rotten about passing them by.

He had gone hardly a mile when he saw the same scene up ahead— a car on the shoulder of the road, two figures lifting their arms.

It occurred to him that he was seeing things that weren't there. Was the rain playing tricks on him? Or was it his conscience? He suddenly feared that he would come upon apparition after apparition if he didn't go back.

There were no lights coming in either direction. George slowed again, almost to a stop, then veered to the right, gathering enough space to make a U-turn across the two-lane highway. He drove thoughtfully as he retraced the distance, half expecting the car to have disappeared.

He was remembering the morning long ago. He had been no more than seven or eight. A hobo had come to the door asking for something to eat. His mother had explained to the man in her nicest voice that she was sorry but it was Sunday and she was on her way to church. Then, as soon as she had closed the door and started back into the house for her hat and gloves, she had halted and touched her forehead. George had been there and he recalled it distinctly. She had said, "Wait a minute—what are my priorities?" She had flown back to the door, prepared to make pancakes or whatever the man desired, but the man had vanished. She had taken to the sidewalk in one direction and she had sent George in the other direction. Neither of them had found the man. His mother had lamented that day until the day she died. "I just know it was the Lord," she would say.

George was relieved to find the Ford still looming there in the rain, and the two figures emerging from it. He pulled back across the highway. He stopped hood to hood.

The male was approaching as George opened the door.

"Trouble?" George asked.

"You wouldn't happen to have a jack would you?" the male asked.

The female—if that was the correct classification—remained in the watery background.

George said, "I just might."

He turned up his collar against the rain and ducked his head and walked toward the rear of the Buick. He opened the trunk and leaned into it to get the jack.

"Merry Christmas," came the voice of the male. Then George felt the blow to his skull, and that was all he felt.

"How long have I been here?" George asked.

"Nine days," Margaret said, squeezing his hand.

"What happened?"

Margaret told him.

"I don't remember anything," he said.

"That's the mercy of God," Margaret said. "Who wants to remember being hit on the head and stuffed in a trunk?"

She went out of the room and came back with a nurse.

"Well, look who's awake," the nurse said brightly. "It's about time!" She busied herself checking his wound.

CHAPTER NINE

"She's been taking excellent care of you," Margaret said.

"Look at it this way," the nurse said. "I always like a challenge. You, sir, are lucky to be alive."

Her use of the word "lucky" reminded George that he was a Presbyterian preacher. A staunch Presbyterian shied from that adjective, preferring good fortune to be identified with providence not luck, but George wasn't going to make a point of it now. Just lying there trying to put his world back together was all he could handle.

"How much longer will I be here?" he inquired.

"That depends on how good a boy you are," the nurse told him. "You've only been out of the intensive care unit for two days. We don't want to rush things."

"My George is always a good boy," Margaret said. She lifted his hand and kissed it.

The nurse was on her way out. She told them she was writing a note to the doctor to prepare him for the good news.

❀ ❀ ❀

Little by little, George caught up with his life. Now that he could have company, the flow of people in and out was fairly steady. Sweet Martha—he couldn't place her at first—brought him up to date on Dusty and thanked him for getting Robert Ashton to take the case. She told him that Wilma was losing ground. "I don't think she'll make it if things don't go right for Dusty."

"Things will go right for Dusty," George said.

"God knows," Sweet Martha said, "I don't."

George liked her flat-out honesty. He hoped to some-day be the mature Christian that she was.

When Robert Ashton came to visit him, George pumped him about the upcoming trial. The attorney made no promises about the outcome.

"We must get you well so you can come and take the stand."

"Will they let a man with a hole in his head take the stand?"

Brief laughter.

"You should be proud of me," Ashton said. "I've been thinking a lot about the Resurrection recently."

"Oh? And where do you stand as of now?"

"You know how the discrepancies in the four Gospels have put me off? Well, they still do—but there's no doubt that the Gospel writers wanted us to believe, and so I'm wondering why they didn't get together to get their stories straight. Surely it wasn't their intention to confuse the issue. The very fact that there was no collusion on their part, that they trusted their own truths—"

"Interesting point."

"—is worth thinking about. If witnesses deliver packaged identical stories, with no rough edges, you can be pretty sure you're dealing with fiction somewhere."

"Right up a lawyer's alley," George said. "Tailor-made

for your kind of brain. But remember this—when faith happens, it will be in your heart and not in your mind."

Bill Taylor stuck his head in the door. George motioned him in, and behind Bill Taylor came Harry Beckham. George introduced them to Robert Ashton, who said he was just leaving.

"We've seen you in church, haven't we?" Bill Taylor gave Ashton's hand a thorough shaking.

"I'm not a regular," Ashton said.

"He will be someday," George put in.

"Have you been coming recently?" Harry Beckham asked.

"No, I'm afraid not—not recently," Ashton confessed.

"That's a shame," Harry Beckham said. "You've been missing out. Bill here has been bringing some mighty fine sermons."

Ashton was gone.

Harry Beckham looked at George. "I believe somebody's making progress."

"Yes," Bill Taylor said. "What a difference. I suspect you don't even remember my last visit."

George didn't.

As for making progress, George figured he was. But at the moment he felt so tired he couldn't be sure.

🌼 🌼 🌼

"The dogwood trees are blooming," Lindley said.

"Say," George said, "that's an idea—a poem about dogwoods."

"I think everybody is going to write about dogwoods. I want to write something *different*."

There she sat, pencil and tablet in hand, looking to George for help with inspiration. Behind her, on the wide windowsill, was a veritable garden, florist variety.

"Let's see," he said. "A springtime poem about something different."

"I thought about writing one about mums—I like mums—but Mother says that mums are a fall flower."

If left to themselves, George thought, yes. But there on the windowsill a purple chrysanthemum was thriving, thanks to a nursery's know-how. Actually, it was the only member of the assembly that seemed to be holding its own. Even the most recent cut flowers were on toward wilting and should soon follow the other retirees. The potted green plant looked as if it might be getting too much sun.

"I have an idea," George said.

Lindley waited.

"Maybe," he said, "you can do something with this." He made a fist with his right hand and cupped it in his left. He was thinking.

"With what?" Lindley asked.

"I've had a lot of flowers in this hospital room, but it never was really springtime until you came in."

Lindley closed her eyes and was the picture of contemplation.

George thought his idea was pretty good. Could she do something with it? It was awfully sentimental, he supposed, but what was wrong with a little sentimentality at her young age? Or, for that matter, at his advanced age? He guessed that all-in-all he was sentimental.

Of course, some people thought that belief in the empty tomb was utter sentimentality. He felt for them. He could see the difficulty in accepting the notion that good had already triumphed over evil. Especially could he see it now. On the other hand, he suspected that many believers did embrace sentimental lies—did find the stable quaint, and the thorns and the cross but symbols. They believed, but not substantially. *Please God,* he thought, *I am not one of them—am I?*

Lindley had crossed her legs and was using her knee as a base for her tablet as she wrote and erased and wrote and erased some more.

Finally she said, "I think I have it now. It's only two sentences, but my teacher says it can be as long or as short as we want."

"Good."

"Are you ready?"

"Sure am."

"My father is in the hospital. He has flowers that bloom. But he says it isn't springtime till I come in the room."

"Hey, sweetie, that is really good."

It really was, George thought.

❀ ❀ ❀

"Have you heard the news?" Margaret said, sweeping into his room. Margaret was not one who swept into rooms.

"What news?" George had been reading his Bible. He laid his Bible aside.

"They caught them—the couple."

"Thank God!" he said. He picked the Bible up again and slammed it back down on the bed. Then, as if he might have exuberated too quickly, he asked if they were sure they had the right ones.

"They've already confessed, but someone is bringing you a photo spread just the same."

George wondered if he could identify the couple. They were white and he guessed them to be somewhere in their twenties, and that was about all the help he could be.

"I hope the confessions don't mean a plea bargain," he said.

"If you had died in that trunk, they would be facing murder charges. That needs to be emphasized."

"I hope they throw the book at them."

The couple had abandoned the Buick behind an old motel on Lamar, where they had "swapped" it for a Cadillac. The motel had fallen from grace in the '70s, but the Cadillac was brand new, George was told. There was a story in the contrast, but George had more to dwell on than that. He remembered passing the couple on the highway and then, at the prospect of apparitions, turning back. Oh, yes, he remembered that the man was short, that he wore no hat, that his sopping tangled hair hid his forehead. What he could not remember, what haunted him and eluded him, was what the man had said from behind him when he opened the trunk.

It came back to him in an instant when the officer placed the photo spread before him.

"Merry Christmas," came out of him as he pointed to one of the men.

The officer didn't understand the greeting.

"He's the one," George said. "I couldn't have described him to you except for the rat's nest over his forehead, but that's the guy right there."

Merry Christmas. George wished he had not remembered it. Certainly he wished he had not repeated it. Under the circumstances, those words sounded pointedly sacrilegious.

Joel Scotney stood beside the bed, preparing to leave. He shook George's hand and then held it captive.

Joel had made regular visits. It happened that most of them had occurred when nobody else was there. Vaguely George wondered if that was by shrewd planning on Joel's part or purely providence. On one visit George had taken the opportunity to tell Joel his new and still fuzzy thoughts about male friendships. How physical closeness might fulfill a need that oftentimes is perceived as erotic. How those who had missed out on a father's embraces might, with a surrogate, be able to catch up and deal objectively with their troubled identities.

No sooner had George articulated these thoughts than he began to think how easily this approach could backfire.

Today the subject had not come up—not until now. And even now, not with words—only with a clasp of hands.

"When do you plan to break out of here?" Joel asked.

"They tell me I'm going home in three days if that last skin graft heals."

"You must be eager to get back in the pulpit."

"Yes and no. But remember I'm on a three-month leave of absence. It'll be a while before I'm in the saddle again."

"You play golf?"

"I try," George said, "that's about it. You?"

"Never held a club. Would you like to give me some lessons when you're up and at 'em again?"

George smiled. "I believe that could be arranged."

CHAPTER NINE

Margaret came into the room, and Joel let go of George's hand.

CHAPTER 10

$\mathcal{I}$t was weeks before Margaret said anything to George about it. When she did bring it up, she was straightforward. They sat facing each other over after-dinner coffee in the country French atmosphere at Paulette's. What was going on, she wanted to know, between him and Joel Scotney?

Joel had called that afternoon.

"We were setting up a golf game for tomorrow. Joel wants me to teach him, if you can believe that."

"That's not what I mean," Margaret said.

George had spotted three members of Memorial Presbyterian scattered throughout the restaurant. Little salutes had been sent back and forth. Here came two more members, James and Wendy Kelly. The host was seating them at the next table. Before sitting down, they came over with greetings.

James was jovial. "You'd better get back in the pulpit soon, or all of your patients will get well."

George never knew what to do with remarks like that.

When the Kellys had retreated to their table, George asked Margaret if she was ready.

"I still have coffee," she said

So did he, but he was ready to leave. He didn't push it, though.

"What is this question about Joel?" he said. "As I've told you, Joel is concerned about his sexual identity. I've been counseling him for a good while."

"Yes, I know."

"I should never have mentioned it to you in the first place. It was highly unethical on my part."

"It seems to me," Margaret said, "that your ministry now—your ministry to Joel Scotney—has gone beyond the bounds of propriety."

"Can't we talk about this in the car?"

"More coffee?" the waiter said.

"Yes, please," Margaret answered.

"—Me too, I guess," George said, pushing his own cup an inch or two toward the waiter.

When he and Margaret were alone again, as alone as possible in Paulette's on a busy night, he placed his elbows on the table and leaned forward for increased intimacy. He tried to tell Margaret his new theory without relating how his personal involvement began.

Margaret's eyes told George that she was confused.

"Propriety," he echoed belatedly, reflectively. "I don't believe I've heard that word since my mother died."

"I'm beginning to think it died with her." Margaret reached into her handbag. Out came an envelope, from which she produced a letter. "Speaking of your mother," she said, "here is a letter I received from one of her friends."

She handed the letter to George.

The country French atmosphere of Paulette's, which struck one as authentic, lost character. Suddenly he and Margaret and the other diners were back in Memphis. The lines of handwriting moved across the sheet of pink stationery as neatly as if the writer had used a ruler for a guide. George turned the page over, his eyes racing ahead for the signature.

There was none.

"I've made it a rule," he said, "not to read any letter without a signature. Life is too short." He put the letter on the table.

"If you don't read it, I shall read it for you," Margaret warned him.

"Go ahead, my sweet," he told her.

Margaret read aloud: *"I have agonized in prayer whether to write this letter or not. I am ill at ease writing it but, my dear, as one who remembers your mother-in-law fondly, I would be less at ease withholding something that required attention. The evening after your father-in-law's funeral I made a batch of fudge and I was more pleased*

*than usual with the outcome, so I decided to take some over
to the house. I was afraid it might be too late, but the lights
were on and I barged up the porch steps. The blinds were
open and I glanced through the living room window. Your
husband and some young man-friend of his sat there on the
couch entwined. Yes, my dear, entwined, and I can assure
you that the man-friend was not family. I have known this
family forever. I did not ring the bell. I thought I was going
to throw up. I proceeded down the porch steps and tossed the
fudge into the shrubbery. George comes from the finest stock.
I can't imagine how this has happened. And him a man of
God! I don't report this to upset you, but to stir you into
action. My prayers are with you. Sincerely, Someone Who
Cares.*

"Probably Alberta Wilcox," George said.

"It makes no difference who wrote it," Margaret stated. "What I want to know is what do you have to say for
yourself?"

A couple from Memorial Presbyterian was about to
pass their table, leaving. George fought for their names.
He drew a blank. He made it a point to address members by their names. It always irked him when he
couldn't.

"Salutations," he said to them.

Margaret said, "Phil and Kitty Blanchard—good to
see you."

The Blanchards responded briefly and were on their
way. They seldom attended services and George was able

to forgive himself for the lack of recall. It occurred to him that they didn't even know he had been out of the pulpit recently. At least he didn't have to deal with questions about it. Or cutesy remarks.

Nothing further was spoken between George and Margaret until they approached Margaret's Volvo in the parking lot. George said he thought he'd drive. He hadn't driven since he received the wound in the head. He thought it was time he got back behind the wheel.

Margaret remonstrated. He wasn't supposed to drive again till after his next checkup.

"I think the doc is being overly cautious," George said, getting in on the passenger side.

"I'm glad that somebody is being cautious about *something*," Margaret said, and turned the key in the ignition.

Their silence returned, the motor humming beneath it. It was not a comfortable silence.

After a while, as they traveled east on Poplar, George dealt with the scene the letter writer had glimpsed through the window. He told Margaret how Joel had left and come back. He told her about the confession and how Joel had gone to pieces.

George was looking straight ahead, not at Margaret.

"I reached out to him," he said, "as I believe you would have reached out to him."

Margaret drove and said nothing.

"As I believe Christ would have reached out to him."

Against the silence he dared to add, "As I believe Christ *did* reach out to him."

"Are you sure that's not blasphemy or something?" Margaret said.

There was no rancor in her voice. It was as though she asked simply for information.

❀ ❀ ❀

It happened that Joel Scotney was "entertaining a cold" on the Saturday the golf game was set. When he called to cancel, he sounded stuffed up and miserable but in a mood to talk. George, alone in the house, lay down on the couch with the telephone at his ear.

He didn't have to put out a bit of effort to keep the conversation going. Joel told him about a call he'd received from a high school friend back home in Little Rock. The friend, Reeve, a CPA, had been hired by a Memphis firm and would soon be moving. Reeve had told Joel he'd finally faced the fact that he was gay and he thought it would be easier to start his new life in a new locality.

George asked, "Had you and he ever discussed this proclivity —yours or his—before?"

"No."

"He just threw it out there bald-faced?"

"Just like that."

"Had you ever suspected?"

"No."

"Not even an inkling?"

"Well-l-l—maybe an inkling," Joel said. "I confess that if a man is nice looking, I sometimes catch myself toying with the idea."

"But if I've understood you before, this doesn't mean that you're necessarily attracted to that individual."

"That's right. I think maybe it's just a case of misery loving company."

"You said that, I didn't," George made clear.

"I fess up to it," Joel said.

"Was he married?"

"A divorce is underway."

Another marriage torn apart. The sadness of amputation was everywhere. Last year there had been so many divorces in his congregation that George had come to think of himself as someone whose job was to pick up pieces of bodies at a crash site. Now whenever he heard of another divorce, whether he knew the parties or not, something inside of him despaired.

Joel was telling him that Reeve said his wife was understanding. "Fortunately, there were no children."

"Fortunately," George echoed.

He thought of the teenager he knew, who every week spent four days with his mother and three days with his father. The boy carried his stuff in grocery sacks and a duffle bag, and now that he was old enough to drive, lived mostly out of the trunk of his Toyota. He had said to George, "I feel like I'm visiting everywhere I go." He had said it without seeming to blame anyone.

"Here's my problem," Joel was saying. "Before Reeve came across with all of this, I invited him to hang out here until he finds a place to live. It was after that that he told me—I guess he was giving me an opportunity to back out if I wanted to. But what a hypocrite I would have been."

"Would have been. I take it you didn't withdraw the invitation."

"No, I didn't. If there's one thing I dislike, it's self-righteousness."

There was silence while George turned the matter over in his mind. He sat up on the couch, as though he would be able to think better in an upright position.

"I hear what you're saying," he said, "but if you're serious about the things we've discussed, I advise you to find some way out of this. Surely you can think of something."

"You mean lie?"

George was caught and he didn't like the feeling. "It's just that I think you'd be making a mistake if—"

"Then you do mean lie," Joel stated.

"—Not necessarily," George said, stealing moments to compose an answer. "You might just tell this friend the truth—about yourself, about your decision to take the other road. Just tell him you think it would be unwise at this point—"

"Yeah," Joel said.

But his tone was ponderous and he made no promises.

George, whose Bible reading had faltered since the death of Rose Templeton, reprimanded himself for his slackness. In response, he set out to read the Gospels straight through. Once he had begun, the burden of his conscience lightened, and he found that he was not reading from a sense of failed obligation but from sheer hunger for the Word.

He chose the Gospels because he felt weak in them. In seminary he had received a strong foundation in the Old Testament and a thorough schooling in the Letters of the New Testament—not to mention being steeped in systematic theology. Of course there had been instruction in the life of Christ. But it was less intense, and George had ho-hummed his way through it as if he'd covered all of that in his childhood Sunday School classes. Accordingly, in his years of preaching he had stuck mostly with the Old Testament and the New Testament Letters. He realized now that he had even taken pride in those approaches, feeling that they gave depth to the study of Christ. The truth was, he knew the doctrines about Christ better than he knew Christ himself.

So he read the four Gospels as he had never read them

before. The general labels were there in his subconscious: Matthew presenting the promised one as a king; Mark, as a servant; Luke, as a man; John, as God. But he attempted to read with no thought of categories, no studious analyzing. He let the story sweep over him as it would, and that way it was practically new. When he came to the words of Jesus, he found he was not only reading them, he was listening to them.

The scenes came alive. The shepherds smelled of sheep, the fishermen smelled of fish. The feet of Jesus were dusty. He became so real that George could picture him walking behind an olive tree to relieve himself. Usually his eyes burned with gentleness, but sometimes they burned and were not gentle at all.

George was in the synagogue in Nazareth the day that Jesus stood to read. The scroll of the Prophet Isaiah was handed to Jesus, and George heard him read, "The spirit of the Lord is on me, because he has anointed me to preach good news to the poor. He has sent me to proclaim freedom for the prisoners and recovery of sight for the blind, to release the oppressed, to proclaim the year of the Lord's favor." George heard the hush that followed. "Today," Jesus said, "this Scripture is fulfilled in your hearing." The hearers looked at each other, astonished. An uproar ensued, and it was understandable. This was a carpenter's son. George tagged along as they drove Jesus out of town. They were planning to throw him off the nearby cliff, but he walked right through the crowd and went on his way. George had to smile. It seemed that sometimes Jesus had been just that elusive with him.

He listened to the parables with a freedom he had never enjoyed previously. The Lord told some pretty good stories, he decided. It occurred to him that stories could be fiction and still be truer than true—the Prodigal Son for instance. George certainly didn't think it was a factual story, and yet he didn't doubt that it had happened millions of times. He imagined that the father was waiting and the feast was ready for preparation in every town, in every hamlet, at any given hour.

He started to skip the Good Samaritan, but that wouldn't have been fair. It was impossible for George to read it— to hear it—without thinking of Rose Templeton.

The enormity of the Lord's demands came down upon him when he heard him say, "Love your enemies. Do good to those who hate you, bless those who curse you, pray for those who mistreat you. If someone strikes you on the cheek, turn to him the other also."

It was completely unreasonable. Jesus couldn't mean that. George had always explained it away the best he could, but now he didn't try. He didn't plan to become a pacifist, but he no longer would say that the Lord didn't mean what he said. There it was—you either took it seriously or you didn't.

"I was . . . in prison, and you did not visit me," the Lord said at one point.

Which reminded George that he should visit Dusty Case. He had missed a week. On the last occasion, as on the first, Dusty had asked him to please bring him some whiskey, just enough to wash his mouth out with.

George was actually considering it. There was so little that one could do to gladden another's heart. What would be the harm? Well, for one thing, he would damage his own integrity. But then the Christian thing might be to give up one's integrity in order to commit a kindness. But in the long run it wouldn't be a kindness, would it? The quenching would be so brief, and it would only intensify the desire.

What stopped him, of course, was the simple fact that he would not be able to get away with it. He could put a swig or two in a small medicine bottle, but the guard—probably the black female he wouldn't want to mess with—would seize it.

He was driving down Poplar toward the jail when he realized what he should do. What he should have done already. He turned around and drove to the church, said hello to those in the office, and went to the cabinet where the "private" communion case was kept. He placed the bread in the container, poured the "wine" in the small flask. He had always been put off by the fact that his brand of Presbyterianism substituted grape juice for wine. In George's opinion, the blood of Christ might avail in plain grape juice, but its expression deserved the finest vintage wine affordable. On the way back, he stopped at a liquor store on Poplar to buy a bottle of red wine. He asked for the most expensive they had. Upon hearing the price, he backed down considerably. He bought the most expensive he could afford. He went to the Buick, opened the communion case, poured out the grape juice on the grass bordering the pavement. He had to go back inside the store to borrow a corkscrew. He was inept with the corkscrew. After a struggle, he managed to open the bottle. He filled the flask and spilled some of the wine and was glad that the wine had not yet been consecrated.

Inside the Buick, before starting the motor, George turned the bottle up and took a swallow. Then he looked around, hoping that no one had seen him. Not only had his indiscretion been totally out of character for a Presbyterian minister, drinking alcoholic beverages in an automobile was against the law.

There was something else he had to worry about. By Presbyterian order, a minister was supposed to have a church elder along with him when he took communion to a shut-in. George could just imagine what Harry Beckham would say about his disregard of the dictum, and also about the use of real wine, though Harry himself was no teetotaler.

When he parked at the jail, George transferred the paper-bagged bottle of wine to the trunk of the Buick.

He caught sight of Joel Scotney's overcoat and excavat-ed it from the trunk. He put it beside the driver's seat. On the homeward trip he might stop by and return it to Joel. Joel had probably forgotten all about the coat, but there it was and George had told Dusty he would return it.

The communion case and his Bible were about the same size. Carrying both, George presented himself to the desk. From there he was shown to the chaplain's office for the purpose of this particular visit. He placed the case and his Bible on the table and remained stand-ing until Dusty was let in.

"I brought the Sacrament," George said, explaining the small black case.

Dusty didn't understand.

"The Lord's Supper," he said, opening the case. "Perhaps you've always called it Communion."

"I've never called it anything," Dusty said.

"You or your grandmother told me that you were bap-tized when you were a boy. At Bible camp, I believe. Have you never received Communion?"

"They used to pass it around at the tabernacle," Dusty remembered aloud. "When I was little and wanted some, they wouldn't let me, and then when I was older I didn't want it."

"You confessed to me that you didn't 'hold on to Jesus' while you were in Nam. Listen, Dusty, I can understand that. But it's clear you were drifting away before you left home." George had not yet taken the elements from the open case. With both hands, palms up, he gestured to them. "Dusty, this helps us hold on to Jesus."

"I don't see how," Dusty said.

"I don't see how either," George said, "but I believe it."

He went on to give Dusty a brief and helpless course in the mystery of the body and blood of Christ.

The guard was a man this time. He pulled from his back pocket a paperback, a mystery of a different kind, and began to read.

George pointed out to Dusty that the Sacrament was for believers only. He then said the Apostle's Creed and asked Dusty if he believed these things were true.

Dusty, who had been gazing at the elements the whole time, looked up at George, straight in the eyes. He said, "I believe those things are true if you tell me they are."

Suddenly George experienced a feeling of almost terror. His responsibility as a minister of the Gospel enlarged in his throat and, for a moment, he thought it was going to choke him. He wanted to say to Dusty, *"No—no—no*—that's not how it works. You must believe these things for yourself, with your own heart, with your own intellect. I'm not God, I'm not all-knowing, I'm not right about everything." But how could he say that at this particular point? Would it not be at odds with the purpose at hand?

Whatever the risk, the Sacrament was before him and he had to speak the truth. He looked straight into Dusty's eyes and said, "I'm not right about everything."

"I'll trust you just the same, if that's all right with you." Dusty gave him a wink.

The wink did not seem at all proper, but neither did the circumstances, neither did the surroundings.

As he poured from the flask into the cup, George mentioned to the waiting communicant the necessity of confession. "Not to me, to God. Just bow your head and confess your sins privately."

Dusty didn't bow his head right away. He waited awhile and looked at the wall. Then he crossed his arms on the desk and lay his head on his arms, forehead down. Shortly, he sat up and said, "I can't do it."

"I have a general prayer of confession," George said. "I'll say it aloud and you can repeat after me—"

"No," Dusty said. He pointed to the sacrament. "I mean I can't do that."

"Why not? Do you think you're not good enough? I'm not good enough either. People who think they're good enough are not welcome at the Lord's Supper. This table is for sinners. For sinners who know their need."

Dusty was shaking his head slowly from side to side. "I killed Mrs. Templeton," he told George.

"You didn't kill Mrs. Templeton. You told me what happened. How it happened. I believe you."

"No. You're not listening to me. What I'm saying now is I killed her."

"Not on purpose, though."

"I shouldn't have touched her whiskey. It wouldn't have happened if I hadn't got drunk. So, the way I see it, I'm guilty."

No, George thought, I'm the one who is guilty. I preached the sermon that started the chain of events. He thought about the complexity of it all. There was no such thing as simple truth. If one held with predestiny and the sovereignty of God the way a Presbyterian was supposed to, God himself was the perpetrator. George recalled that the mother of Samuel in the Old Testament had stated in her prayer, "The Lord kills and makes alive."

He bowed his head and said aloud, "Lord, make us alive."

After assuring Dusty that it was proper for him to receive, he opened the Bible and read aloud, "The Lord Jesus, on the night he was betrayed, took bread, and when he had given thanks, he broke it and said, 'This is my body'...took the cup, saying, 'this cup is the new covenant in my blood.'"

George realized that until now Dusty Case had been to him like a one-dimensional cutout, more a type than a person. How very little they had talked that night as they walked down Poplar with the traffic whizzing by. How very little they had talked at all. Or, how poorly

George had actually listened. What was it Rose Templeton had said after taking his sermon to heart? "It's not that we set out to be haughty. We just don't see them. We just don't look." *We just don't hear them,* George added.

Dusty came into focus at the taste of the wine. His Adam's apple bobbed as he swallowed. He ran his tongue slowly over his lips, not obscenely but with obvious pleasure.

"That was good all the way down to my toes," he said.

George assumed that the two who abducted him were being held in this same facility. He was thankful he didn't have to visit them. Perhaps if he knew that they were believers in Jesus and truly repentant, perhaps he might force himself to, but the thought of administering the Lord's Supper to them was repugnant to his very core.

The thought followed him outside the jail. A sudden nausea drove him into the small grassy courtyard of the Lutheran church next door. He sat on the bench and hung his head between his knees.

After awhile, the pastor of the church came into the courtyard and asked if he was all right.

"Yes," George lied.

On the way home, he stopped at Joel Scotney's apartment to return the overcoat that had been in the trunk of the Buick all this time. It was Saturday afternoon and Joel's BMW was nosed into its slot.

George rang the bell. He was feeling better now.

Joel Scotney answered. Taking the coat, he invited George inside.

"Oh, I'd better be getting on home," George said.

"There's someone I want you to meet—Reeve Malone, my friend from Little Rock I was telling you about."

Joel's hand tugged at George's elbow.

"Reeve," Joel said to the young man rising from the white wicker settee, "this is my pastor, George McKenna."

Reeve Malone would have looked like your typical accountant if he had been wearing a suit and tie, George thought.

He was wearing a white terry cloth bathrobe. "Pardon my dishabille," he said, shaking hands with George.

George wondered if that was what Reeve Malone called a bathrobe. "How are you, Mr. Malone?"

Joel pushed one of the black safari chairs under George.

"I've been telling Reeve," Joel was saying, "about our relationship—your theory about the touching. Better if it comes from you, though."

George wanted to touch Joel all right. He wanted to

kick his butt. This subject was something between them, nothing he was ready to discuss with a stranger. It seemed to be required of him, however, and he began to articulate as best he could his hopes that a surrogate father's embraces, though belated, might help to make a man a man.

And that's how he put it, "to make a man a man."

Reeve Malone took offense. He kept his composure, didn't say anything right away, but George could see that something was coming.

Joel changed the subject, but it wouldn't stay changed.

Reeve Malone said to George, "Then if I tell you I'm gay, I'm not a man—is that your position?"

"Come on, guys, let's not get into this," Joel said.

"You brought it up," Reeve Malone reminded him.

"My position," George said, "would be that you're not fulfilling your sexuality in the way that God intended when he created us male and female."

"If you're going to bring God into this—and I realize that, as a preacher, you have to—then I ask you, would God have me lie? It happens that I am homosexual, and let me tell you I've been living a lie ever since I was fourteen. A friend used to sneak his father's *Playboy* and share it with me, and I would pretend I was interested. I dated—had a lot of fun—but every so-called serious date I ever had was a lie. My marriage was a lie —I started to say from beginning to end, but no, the end, whatever else you might say about it, was not a lie."

George sent a glance in Joel's direction. Joel was the host and George with his eyes was asking if he should reply or let the matter drop.

The barest shrug came from Joel.

"Would you have God lie?" George asked Reeve Malone. "Is it possible for the intelligence behind the universe to lie? We Christians believe that God has expressed truth in the living word, Jesus Christ, and in the written Word, the Bible. We notice that the Word contains some very strong admonitions about this holy thing we call sex. Should you ever want a rundown on this, I'd be more than happy to get with you."

"Thanks, but I'm very happy with my life at the moment."

George took "at the moment" to be a significant phrase, whether Reeve Malone did or not. "Just thought I'd offer," he said.

"Beer?" Joel said. "I have Sprite also."

George wanted to be going, but he heard himself saying, "Sprite's fine with me."

"You *kno-o-w* what I like, " Reeve Malone said.

"One Sprite, one beer, coming up."

The window toward Overton Park was open. Birds cried out from the zoo, sounding of bright colors. Or it might have been the ruckus of siamangs. How they loved to swing from one end of the cage to the other and put on a show. When Lindley was younger, she had always wanted to see the siamangs first, but their screams would frighten her and she would want to hurry on. It had been too long since the family had been to the zoo, George thought.

"You and I are coming at this from opposite poles, I know," Reeve Malone said before Joel returned. "But two things you might want to consider. Number one—my father was very much on the scene when I was growing up, and we had a close, warm relationship."

"I'm glad," George said. He genuinely was glad. Not many sons, regardless of their leanings, ever claimed to have had a close relationship with their father. "What is it they say? The exception proves the rule." George wasn't sure what that meant exactly, but it seemed the thing to say.

Reeve Malone was saying as the beer reached his hand, "Number two—and I'll say it right here in front of our friend Joel—I think what you're going to accomplish in this therapy will be far from what you hope. Which is okay by me, of course. You might fight fire with fire, but you don't fight sex with touching."

"You could be right," George admitted. A swallow of the Sprite was but little refreshment against his depression. The mood had been thickening ever since he'd faced his hatred in the courtyard of the Lutheran church. His hatred for the couple who kidnapped him—it kept overlapping his visit here. "The whole issue is complex. I don't claim to have all the answers. All I know is, I'm trying to help someone who desires help. Joel here asked for help, didn't you, Joel?"

Joel allowed as much. But he said, "Enough of this."

George continued, "If the love of God expressed in human arms won't get it straight, then I'm sunk."

"Get it straight," Reeve Malone repeated, almost smiling. "Is that a pun?"

"I didn't mean it as one," George said, and downed more Sprite.

The host was trying to change the subject, but the newcomer from Little Rock had one more thing he wanted to say to George. "I don't want Joel to live the lie that I did. Spare him that. Spare the woman he might someday marry."

The man had a point. Still, it didn't change the love expressed in the "rules and regs" of the Creator. The opposite, however, was a possibility. George believed that the love of God could change a life, and he said so.

The topic of AIDS had not come up. George started to introduce it, then decided not to. The advice against homosexual activity had been around long before the dread disease made its appearance. That advice was still valid on its own—without scare tactics.

Leaving, he shook hands with Reeve Malone and then put an arm around Joel, squeezed, and said, "See you soon."

Yet he wondered if he would.

Reeve Malone would doubtless have an influence.

And Reeve might be right about the therapy pushing Joel in the other direction. A theory was all it was, and George had thought it worth a try. He still thought it worth a try.

You had to take chances if you wanted to follow Christ.

Perhaps faith wasn't faith at all if it wasn't first an adventure.

The thing that haunted him as he drove home was not the question about Joel Scotney but his responsibilities in regard to his kidnappers. You couldn't embrace radical Christianity in one area and disregard it in another.

Oh, he guessed that you could. He'd been doing it all of his life, hadn't he?

Where was integrity?

Jesus gave no spelled-out instruction in how to help Joel Scotney. He did, however, speak clearly on the other matter—in extreme terms.

The matter of turning one's cheek.

CHAPTER 11

George and Robert Ashton were lunching at Brad's. Once again the topic of conversation was Dusty Case. Ashton had arranged for a plea-bargain that would bring the charge down to involuntary manslaughter.

"All right!" George said, elated.

"Wait," Ashton said. "Are you ready for this? Dusty hasn't made up his mind whether he wants to plea-bargain or not. Says he's *praying* about it."

George had taken a large bite of the barbeque and had to chew a long time to get rid of it. "Praying about it? That's interesting. But he'd be a fool not to plea-bargain, wouldn't he?"

"He would be that," Ashton confirmed. "I told him if he goes to trial he could get murder one or murder two. I warned him he might get the death penalty."

"Do you think he would?"

"I doubt it, but I think he'll get no telling how many years. Why don't you talk some sense into his head?"

George said he would try and then he shifted to something else entirely. He began to pour out his desire that his kidnappers be released into his custody.

"Do you realize," Robert Ashton said, "how difficult that would be?"

"I realize that you're an excellent attorney," George threw back.

"We're talking about, I'd say, one chance in a hundred."

"Fine with me, let's talk about it."

"You didn't ask for my opinion, but I don't think it's a good idea. Are you sure you want to bring this on yourself?"

George refrained from saying, "I'm not sure of anything anymore." It would not have helped his present cause, and Robert Ashton might have applied it to questions about the resurrection of Christ, since that event had been a focal point in previous conversations.

He said, "I'm sure."

Robert Ashton asked him what Margaret thought of the idea.

"She's coming around."

They were leaving Brad's and working their toothpicks seriously.

"Okay," the attorney said. "I'll start the paperwork."

"You're a good man," George said.

"A deal like this will require the consent of the other party. The owner of the stolen Cadillac. Don't count your chickens. All I can promise is, I'll try."

Within an hour, George was sitting across from Dusty.

"Here's how I see it," Dusty said. "I got drunk deliberately. Mrs. Templeton wouldn't have died if I hadn't got drunk. And that's not the only thing. I was planning to kill somebody—me. So I don't think it's right to beg off like nothing was my fault."

"Dusty, you don't grasp—"

"Maybe I've been reading too much in that Bible you brought me."

George couldn't let himself reflect on that for the moment. He said, "The way the system works—"

"What I haven't told you is—now don't laugh at me—I'd like to go to school and learn to be a minister."

"I could never laugh at that," George said, recovering from the impact.

He didn't want to discourage Dusty from that ambition, but neither did he want to build him up with false hopes. Even if the future allowed the possibility, George had his doubts.

Dusty said, "I don't want to start out with something that's not right on my conscience."

"Don't you understand that if you go to trial you could get the death penalty? At best, you'll get years. You won't have the chance to go to school and learn to be a minister. Think about it. Give yourself that chance."

"I didn't make up my mind for sure until a few minutes before you came.'

"Come on, Dusty," George said, "go for the plea-bargain."

"No. It wouldn't be right."

George was moved by Dusty's integrity and yet what else could you call him but a fool? There ought to be a word—perhaps there was one that George couldn't think of—that better expressed that kind of daring. He recognized in Dusty's decision the same practical holiness he had observed in Rose Templeton when she refused to back down from her stand with Christ. He did not feel easy around it.

Dusty, he supposed, would have to do his witnessing where the Apostle Paul did some of his—in prison.

When he got home that afternoon, the house smelled of a pie baking in the oven—apples, cinnamon. To George, the blending of those aromas was one of the delights of the sensual world.

"What a wife I have," he said.

CHAPTER ELEVEN

His wife's hands were involved with sorting the laundry. George kissed the back of her neck, and she relaxed against him for a moment, then proceeded with the chore.

It was true. What a wife he had: good looking, good cook, good fighter, good balancer of the checkbook, good at raising a daughter and making dresses for her, good at everything George could think of, except for unscrewing tight jar caps, and after all, that gave him a chance to save the day now and then.

And yes, she was good in the marriage bed. Nothing wrong with a preacher having a wife who filled the bill in that category. There was indeed something right about it. George had been a virgin when they married, a condition he had deplored but later appreciated, and he had never committed adultery. For those reasons, he could not compare Margaret with other women—not on that score. And 99 percent of the time he had no desire to put himself in a position that would allow it.

The apple pie, not surprisingly, was as good as it smelled.

George took a second slice, saying that he knew he shouldn't. He should go on a diet, he said.

"If you're serious about it, I'll stop the desserts," Margaret said. "I should lose a pound or two myself."

"Daddy," Lindley said, "I don't think you need to diet. I can't even tell that your stomach is getting bigger."

George and Margaret looked at each other and controlled their smiles. Nobody had said anything about his stomach in particular.

The look that passed between them set the mood for the rest of the evening—warm, affectionate, a hint of humor. George wanted to tell Margaret about Dusty and the plea-bargain, and about Ashton's agreement to take on the custody request, but he didn't want the mood to change. The act of love was in the air, and he didn't want to bring up the other matters until the promise was fulfilled.

So it was the next morning before he mentioned that he'd spoken with Robert Ashton. In regard to the plea-bargain, Margaret was speechless. In regard to the other, she wasn't.

"But you haven't even met them yet," she said. "Except for that night, and you certainly can't call that meeting them. You don't know what you're getting into."

Lindley was off to school, and they had the house, the two of them.

"I'd like to think that what I'm getting into is Christianity."

"A sense of balance, George, please. You've always had a sense of balance, until recently. And by the way, what do you plan to do with them?"

"I was hoping—"

She had turned from emptying the dishwasher and

was waiting for him to continue.

"I was hoping maybe you'd agree to offer them the room over the carport."

"If that's what it takes to be a Christian, I'm not sure that I am one."

"Of course, you are. I had the same fight. All I'm asking is that you pray about it."

Margaret dropped a cup.

"I don't have to pray about it," she said. "I know where I stand."

George picked up the larger pieces, and Margaret swept the smaller ones into the dustpan.

Carl and Dee Davenport had dropped out of high school when he was in the eleventh grade and she was in the tenth. They had married soon thereafter, with falsified parental consent for Dee. In her past was a string of foster homes from which she had run away countless times. Carl came from a well-to-do family who had bailed him out of one scrape after another and then, going to the opposite extreme, had kicked him out. He occasionally picked up money by painting houses. More often, he and Dee would lift merchandise from K Mart or WalMart or wherever, and then return the merchandise and finagle a cash refund at the customer service desk. They would party on cheap wine whenever their take permitted. It was on one of those occasions that they stole a car for a joyride in the country and had a flat and waved for vehicles to stop.

Learning of their history, George resolved all the more to give them a new beginning if Robert Ashton could arrange their release. The attorney never once encouraged him to think there was more than the slightest chance.

The preparatory warnings were such that George could hardly believe it when the release was granted. He was silent as he and his counsel left the court. Reality was sinking in, and he realized that a fearful challenge was ahead.

A parting handshake with Robert Ashton. George said, "Christ is risen."

"Today was a miracle all right," Ashton responded. "Of course, your being a member of the clergy didn't hurt."

How George would have liked to hear from this man the proper response: *Christ is risen indeed.* But, after all, it wasn't Easter. Even then he would not have wanted him to say it with unbelief. There was enough of that in the world. There was enough of that in the church.

George hoped to get with Robert Ashton when the Dusty business was behind them. If Robert Ashton didn't get in touch with him, he would make the move himself. He must continue to bear witness regarding the Resurrection.

Oh, to be able to persuade the unpersuaded.

That last thought, after a moment, caused George to smile. It was preposterous to think that he, George McKenna, could come up with words that would change anyone's mind about the most questioned event in history. He guessed what his main duty in this case was to be. If *Robert Ashton does not detect something of the risen Christ in my life,* George thought, *then I have no claim to make.*

And he has no reason to believe.

"I still don't understand," Carl Davenport said.

George was driving. Carl, jockey size, barbered, bearing little resemblance to the man in the rainy dark, sat on the passenger side. Dee, who might have been pretty had she lived another life, sat in the back.

"I told them I would be responsible for you," George said. "It's as simple as that."

George told him that no strings were attached. "I'm a minister, and I represent Jesus Christ."

"We met a minister once," Dee said. "He wanted us for sex—both of us."

All that George could say to that was, "That's not the kind of minister I am."

"See him on the street," Carl said, "and you wouldn't think he was that kind either."

"I can assure you that he wasn't a true representative of Jesus Christ, no matter what he looked like on the street, or in church. There's a whole bunch of counterfeits running loose everywhere."

George was ready to move on from that subject. He really didn't want to know if they had done business with the man or not.

He told them about Sweet Martha. A black lady, he called her, remembering with a sting that his mother and her generation of southerners would never have called a black woman a lady. "She needs her house painted, inside and out," he said to Carl. He found Dee in the rearview mirror and said, "She also needs someone to help her with an old lady invalid who lives there. When I told her about you two, she said you were welcome to come and live with her. She's been fixing up her back room, getting ready for you."

Neither Carl nor Dee looked at ease.

George steered the Buick off Union Avenue onto Cooper Street, heading south toward Cooper-Young. He had told Sweet Martha he would take Carl and Dee to Cafe Olé before delivering them, but she had insisted on preparing supper herself, a special supper for the occasion. After supper, she wanted to take them to a meeting her church was having. George, turning down the street where Sweet Martha lived, mentioned the meeting and said they didn't have to go, of course, but it would be a good way to thank Sweet Martha.

They were welcomed with outstretched arms. Sweet Martha didn't let the couple's hesitancy stop her. She drew Dee into one arm and Carl into the other as if they were children.

They had a trapped look.

"Does somebody round here paint?" Sweet Martha asked brightly.

"Carl's a good painter," Dee said.

"That's what I've heard," Sweet Martha said, giving them both an extra squeeze before releasing them.

She pointed them toward the bed and introduced Wilma Smith, who, from her bank of pillows, nodded at each individually.

George went over to the bed and asked Wilma how she'd been.

With a movement of her hand, she seemed to say, "Don't ask."

"Went to see Dusty the other day," George said.

"My baby boy—how is he?"

"He's going to make it."

"At least I know where he is," the invalid said.

George asked her if she had been doing any dancing recently. The question just came out, and George wished immediately that he had not asked it.

The only answer she gave was a silence from deep in her eyes. It told him the question was unkind, but she would forgive him.

Sweet Martha was showing Carl and Dee around the

house. Everything was going smoothly and yet George already was wondering how wise this was, this whole idea. What if Margaret was right? Was he putting Sweet Martha and Wilma in danger? His part in it all—was it faith or foolhardiness? At this point, the only thing to do was beg God to bless, beg God to bring something good out of something unknown, something victorious out of something chancy.

The telephone rang and Sweet Martha answered it.

Carl sidled up to George and asked if she was for real.

"She's the genuine article. If you've never met a Christian lady before, you've met one now."

The phone call was to let Sweet Martha know that their ride to church had to work late tonight and would not be able to pick them up.

"We don't care anything about going to church anyway," Dee said, looking relieved.

"If we walked into a church," Carl said, "the roof would fall in on us sure as hell."

"Hey, sounds like you're the very one needs to go," Sweet Martha chimed.

George had the solution. He would come back after supper and provide transportation. He would stay for the service himself. Perhaps he could persuade Margaret to come along. They could bring Lindley. It would be educational for Lindley.

On the way home he stopped to use a pay phone.

"Lindley, may I speak with your mother?"

"Hi, Daddy. Just a minute."

George told Margaret he was on the way home and asked if they could eat supper a little early, maybe in the next hour. He explained the occasion and encouraged her to come along.

On the other end of the line, silence.

"Margaret—"

"—I can't believe you've actually gone through with this. Do you realize the position you've put me in? If anything happens to that black woman and the old lady, it will be my fault—my fault because I refused to take your kidnappers into our own situation. No, I'm not coming along! I'm not having anything to do with this!"

"Don't go to pieces in front of Lindley," George pleaded.

"And furthermore, don't bother coming home for supper," Margaret said. "I think Lindley and I will go out to Taco Bell."

❀ ❀ ❀

The service had begun when Sweet Martha and her entourage arrived at the church. Carl and Dee had come along. Sweet Martha's banana pie had loosened them up, and they had come without resisting.

Inside the door an ebony woman in white from hat to shoes greeted them. The church was nearly full, and she pointed to some empty seats far down near the front.

Sweet Martha led the way, holding Dee's hand. George and Carl dragged behind. George spied a pew with enough empty seats about halfway and tried to signal to Sweet Martha that these would do, but she was sailing on as fast as the freight of her body would allow.

When the four of them were seated on the third row, the robed choir stood up as though on cue and began to vibrate to the piano's rhythmic introduction. The director, with both arms poised, looked to the pianist, waited, and then suddenly looked to his singers and his arms were in motion and his body was in motion with his arms. The sleeves of his robe flapped as he bounced. The singers clapped to the beat of the song they sang in praise of God and many of the congregation joined in the clapping and some of them joined in the singing too.

George remembered a church in the Alabama of his childhood. It was Tula's church, Tula the woman who washed and ironed for his family. One Wednesday evening during prayer meeting—it was summer and the light of the day lingered—he and Buddy Whipple had chunked rocks through an open window. Tula saw them and recognized George and came barreling out the door. "Your mama's going to hear 'bout this," she called after them. And his mother, of course, did hear. And he, of course, got tanned by his father, who required that he go to church with Tula the next Wednesday evening and apologize to the whole congregation. Buddy Whipple didn't have to do that, and so he didn't get to see what

George saw. "This is a holy place," Tula had told him. "You don't throw rocks at a holy place. See those things on the wall behind the pulpit?" Suspended on nails were a wheelchair and three pairs of wooden crutches and one metal leg brace. "They're not hanging there just for decoration. Folks who came in lame and hobbling didn't need them when they left." George had told his mother what Tula said, and he had asked, "Do you believe that?"

"No, dear, we're Presbyterians," she had explained.

Even now he wondered how those people had noticed the rocks coming through the window, there was so much going on—like tonight.

Now the music was ending and the clapping was taking over completely. George found that he was clapping with the rest of them. He supposed you couldn't lay your head on Sweet Martha's breast as he once had done and be fully the Presbyterian that you were before. People popped up and down and clapped until the preacher reached the pulpit.

The preacher said, "Reader, read!"

A man on the first row stood up, faced the congregation and read in a strong voice the first verse of the first chapter of the Gospel of John. "In the beginning was the Word, and the Word was with God, and the Word was God."

The preacher then expounded at length on that passage. George was impressed. This man did not shy back from the deepest of mysteries. George didn't know what he had expected. Certainly not something so profound.

"Say amen!" the preacher said when he had finished that verse.

The congregation said, "Amen!"

"Reader, read!"

The reader read the next verse and the preacher expounded on that one. He then called for an amen and commanded the reader to read. And so it went from verse to verse, the reader reading, the preacher preaching, each verse a little sermon in itself. If the amen wasn't loud enough, the preacher would say, "I can't hear you!" That would bring forth a fuller response.

In its own manner, the service was as structured and formal as any George had ever attended. He thought about the Episcopal church where he and Margaret attended whenever they visited her parents in Nashville, Margaret having been brought up as an Episcopalian. Over the years he had come to appreciate the high liturgy. He had incorporated bits of it into his own Presbyterian service, there being no strict rubrics. But he suspected that Margaret still felt she was attending something less than the correct church when she sat in his congregation, and that she on her visits back home felt she was receiving Holy Communion after months of drought. He imagined that the people here tonight would miss their liturgy accordingly if they had to leave it.

Now the reader was on the fourteenth verse: "And the

Word became flesh, and dwelt among us—"

The preacher did not let him finish, but interrupted, echoing those nine words. He took things over from there and his inflections told those assembled that this was the sermon toward which he had been building.

"The Bible tells us, 'Without the shedding of blood, there is no remission of sins.' . . . Why did God have to become flesh? Not just so we could see him. Not just so we could spit on him. No, no, no! God, being spirit, had to become flesh in order to bleed for us! Did you hear me, brothers? Did you hear me, sisters? Spirits don't bleed. God became flesh in order to redeem us, in order to save us from the pit! There was no other way."

A chorus of agreement came from the congregation.

George McKenna had to admit that he had never approached John 1:14 from that angle. That God had become flesh in order to redeem us, yes, but connecting it directly with the necessity of sacrificial blood, that was looking at the Incarnation through a new window. That was looking at the drama close up. He just might use it in a sermon of his own someday.

It caught him by surprise when the preacher jumped to John 17:18, where Jesus said to his father, "As you sent me into the world, I have sent them into the world." His followers. His servants. "Part of our calling," the preacher said, "is to bleed for the sins of the world. Not redemptively. Only Jesus could do that. But think about this—we are called to bleed as his examples.

Some of us, we're going to have to bleed blood. At the very least, some of us are going to have to bleed tears."

The preacher began to wrap it up, but George's mind hung on those points and was still on them during the altar call. George had glanced at Carl and Dee from time to time throughout the message. Their faces had been blank, unreadable.

All the more was he surprised when they stepped out into the aisle and joined those who kneeled at the front. Sweet Martha followed and sank to her knees, drawing Carl and Dee into the spread of her arms as she had done when she first welcomed them. George felt the force that was pulling people to the front. If this was the Holy Spirit, he didn't want to resist but he saw no sense in his traipsing forward. So he responded by kneeling on the floor where he was and holding fast to the back of the pew in front of him. He closed his eyes and offered prayer for Carl and Dee and all of those who packed the area between the front row and the pulpit.

When he opened his eyes, he remained in the same position. He could see Sweet Martha pouring out the Gospel to Carl and Dee. He could hear her voice in the hum of the other voices, but he couldn't distinguish the words. The hum was like the prayer of a river rushing in the mountains. George marveled anew at the "ears" of God. To dwell too long on the thought that God could hear and assimilate many prayers at once—the scene here was but an isolated, passing instance—was to tempt oneself with doubt. George thought of the times that David in the psalms had asked God to "incline your ear unto me." *Unto me.* And God had not faulted him for that selfishness. Because David had been a harpist, George sometimes entertained the analogy of a string player bending over his instrument, listening closely as he tunes it. The hard doctrine there was that God, if the analogy held, tuned his instruments by applying tension and distressing their heartstrings. This in order to produce the melody of prayer that God called incense.

He stayed on his knees until the service was over and most of the people had vanished. Then he pulled up and slid back on the pew. His knees were sore.

Coming toward him now were Carl and Dee, looking drained, and Sweet Martha, sunny as morning.

"These children have some good news to tell you," Sweet Martha said.

"Merry Christmas," George said to them. It just came out.

Suddenly Carl's eyes were swimming.

"It's all right," Sweet Martha said. "It's all right."

CHAPTER 12

It was Tuesday night and George McKenna was preparing the sermon he would preach on Sunday morning. After a three-month absence, he was looking forward to being behind the pulpit again.

So much had happened since he preached last time. He had a lot to say, but how to say it was the problem. How to take Rose Templeton and Dusty Case and Wilma Smith and Sweet Martha and Carl and Dee Davenport and apply the Word of God in such a way that the congregation of Memorial Presbyterian Church would get a glimpse of Christ at work in the world. One thing for sure, he didn't plan to wind up the sermon with the conversion of Carl and Dee. That would be too pat. If he had learned anything in these three months, it was that nothing is quite pat when it comes to the life that Christ is living in our midst.

Rose Templeton had taken a sermon seriously and look what happened to her. Dusty Case had come to a point where he would not compromise an ounce of truth, and he was sure to get a stiffer sentence for it. Wilma Smith had risen from her bed and danced, but the dance had ended. Certainly nothing was pat in Joel's case, nor in Robert Ashton's. There was no knowing which direction Joel Scotney would take, and Robert Ashton was still shying from the empty tomb.

With that thought, the darkness of the trunk of the Buick and the pain in his head came back to him. He remembered the cramped position. He had become quite good at blocking the memory from his mind, but now it took over and the pain and the darkness were one. Eternities had come and gone as he lay trusting, doubting, sleeping, waking, questioning, fearing, slipping deeper and deeper into hell. Until the longed-for light broke upon him with voices, and one of the voices had answered his question, saying, "Today is the third day."

Margaret came in and asked how it was going.

"Slowly."

"You'll get back in the swing of it in no time," she said.

He explained the scope he was going for.

"Please don't bring your kidnappers into it," she said. "I'm still not easy about that situation. The danger those women are in."

"Do you know what Rose Templeton said to me when I tried to reason with her about Dusty? She said, 'I doubt if Christianity is ever safe.' I think she was right."

"But to knowingly put someone in danger—"

George swiveled from the word processor, and his wife sat on his lap.

He said quickly, "At the moment you're putting me in danger—I don't think this chair was made for this kind of duty."

"You!" she said, and remained where she was.

George enfolded her. "Carl and Dee Davenport are living new lives now. Let's keep that in mind. If what we believe about conversion is true, they have new hearts."

"I think you can't always tell about conversion at first. We've seen cases where it didn't last. I think you have to wait awhile before you know whether it's the real thing or not."

George would not have expressed it that way, but he knew what she meant.

"I think my sermon will be titled *Adventurous Christianity.* Ask me what my text will be."

"What will your text be?"

"The seventeenth chapter of John. Where Jesus says to his Father, 'As you have sent me into the world, I send them into the world.' In our day he might say, 'As you sent me into the jungle, I send them into the jungle.' We're not called to a safe and monotonous life. We're called to take chances—like turning the other cheek, like praying for our enemy. Where there's obedience to Christ, there's risk. He said for us to follow him and where did he end up? The cross. Where there's no risk, there's no need for faith."

"I'll be honest with you," Margaret said." I prefer a tamer, more controllable religion."

"Now that you put it that way, perhaps my title should be *Untamed Christianity*. Which do you like best?"

Margaret had risen and was almost to the door, "I'd go with the first. It has a softer pedal."

❦ ❦ ❦

Sweet Martha sat beside Joel Scotney on the front pew. Joel, at George's request, had given her a ride to Memorial Presbyterian. Her presence in the sanctuary had not set off alarms.

Memorial Presbyterian had no black members, but it was not too unusual for a black person to visit, especially when there was an infant baptism in the family of a white employer. From where George sat, at the rear and to the right of the pulpit, he could see in certain faces near the front a mild perplexity because no infant baptism was listed in the bulletin today.

Of course, another matter might have caused the perplexity. No anthem was listed in the bulletin. There was always an anthem right before the sermon. Why was there none this Sunday? Because the pastor had planned something else.

When George stepped up to the pulpit, he told the

congregation he had a special treat for them this morning. With that, he gestured toward Sweet Martha and she stood up. He sat down and she turned around and faced the congregation and, without accompaniment, sang, *"Were you there when they crucified my Lord? Were you there when they crucified my Lord? Oh, oh, sometimes it causes me to tremble—tremble—tremble—Were you there when they crucified my Lord?"*

Sweet Martha's voice was the color of her skin. Against the white of the pews and the white of the congregation and the New England white of the walls, the contrast was profound and moving. *"Were you there when they nailed him to the cross? Were you there when they nailed him to the cross? Oh, oh, sometimes it causes me to tremble—tremble—tremble—Were you there when they nailed him to the cross?"*

Whether from shock or from the power of the Holy Spirit, the listeners sat enrapt. George sent a glance around the church. He fully expected to find some disapproving gazes cast in his direction, but every eye was on Sweet Martha. Good. He had taken a chance and God was blessing.

"Were you there when they laid him in the tomb? Were you there"—they were there right now, George reflected—*"Oh, oh, sometimes it causes me to tremble—tremble—tremble—Were you there when they laid him in the tomb?"*

In the darkness of Sweet Martha's throat came a rumbling. Was the earth not quaking beneath the foundation of the church? Sweet Martha's knees bent and she began to sink as if overcome by a flood of grief. Then, before she was too deeply in a squat, the darkness turned to light and she gathered her heft and stood full stature and sang of the Resurrection—sang with all the stops out.

George raised the back of his fist to wipe a tear from his eye. If someone saw, that was fine with him.

—*"Oh, oh, sometimes it causes me to tremble—tremble— tremble—Were you there when he rose up from the grave?"*

George had warned Sweet Martha that there would be no applause. It wasn't the Presbyterian way, he had explained. In the first moment of the silence that followed the last word of the song, he was tempted to rise and clap his hands and motion for the congregation to join him. He felt that most of the members would loosen up to it, but he couldn't be sure and he didn't want a halfhearted response. Also, there was George's own philosophy that musical performances in church were offerings to God and not entertainment. After visiting Sweet Martha's church he had melted on that somewhat, and yet for himself he still preferred the dignity of silence.

Sweet Martha had prepared the way for the sermon. Now it was up to George to deliver it. He stepped up to the pulpit, made no comment on Sweet Martha's special number, read the text and began to preach with a freedom and a buoyance he had never experienced before. While he always trusted the Holy Spirit to speak through him, this was the was the first time he had ever been so conscious of divine assistance. He followed his notes, but he found that he was introducing new points and new analogies and suddenly remembered references as he went along, and they fit and they served well.

"This kind of love is risky," he said, and he happened to be looking toward Rose Templeton's empty spot. "This kind of love is costly."

He shifted to Harry Beckham. "We have created a Jesus who has called us to do nothing out of the ordinary. This Jesus is not the Jesus of the Gospel. This is not the Jesus who said, 'Follow me.' This is not the Jesus who bled for our redemption. I'm afraid that the real Jesus has been absent from our churches for a long time."

When George looked down at the front pew, he saw that Sweet Martha was nodding off to sleep. He and Joel Scotney exchanged amused glances. It's probably my dull delivery, George thought. Or she had listened long enough to make sure he was preaching the true Gospel and now she could relax confidently and snooze through the rest.

"Will we follow the civilized Jesus we hold in our minds? Or the radical Jesus of Nazareth? Will we follow the one who never disturbs? Or the one who burst from the grave and has been doing shocking things ever since? The Jesus who lets us off the hook completely? Or the one who rescues us in order for us to be involved in his mysterious ways? Let us choose this day whom we will serve."

George closed with an unplanned cautioning prophecy. "My friends, I warn you, if you try to follow Jesus in your daily lives and no one criticizes you, you probably aren't following Jesus. I'll make that stronger. If you try to follow Jesus and no *Christian* criticizes you, you probably aren't following Jesus."

"What do you think?" George asked.

"What am I supposed to think?" Margaret said.

"Did I communicate *anything?*"

"Yes, I'm afraid so."

Laura told him how good it was to have him back in the office. Laura was not a member of Memorial Presbyterian. She was a Baptist. Nevertheless, in honor of George's return, she had come yesterday morning to hear him preach.

"What a sermon," she said.

"Do you really think so?"

Usually George didn't fish around like this, but so little had been said to him at the door after the service that he did long for feedback.

"Oh, *my*," Laura said, and that was all he got.

CHAPTER TWELVE

George was going over a stack of matters with Bill Taylor. Things that Bill had put aside until George's return.

"Am I glad you're back," Bill threw in.

"From all I hear, you did a great job," George said.

Laura buzzed him with a call from Lindley.

"Should I leave for a few minutes?" Bill asked.

George told him it wasn't necessary, and picked up the receiver.

"Daddy?"

"Hi, sweetie."

"Mother says for me to ask you if I can go with Kate Russell and her father to see the Peabody ducks this afternoon?"

Margaret usually handled decisions on that order herself. George supposed she had referred their Lindley to him because he had promised on several occasions that he would take her to the famous attraction in the lobby of the Peabody Hotel. It was the sort of thing that residents of Memphis were less likely to visit than tourists. Especially since the old landmark was all the way downtown and the citizens of East Memphis prided themselves on needing very little within the Parkways. George felt guilty about his broken word, and the guilt increased when he told her it would be best if she waited and they went together as a family. He wanted her memory to be of him taking her. He didn't say that, of course, but that was how he felt even though he knew it was selfish.

"We'll do it soon," he assured her.

His daughter's silence sounded as if she didn't believe him.

He asked to speak with her mother. He explained his decision to Margaret. "And besides," he said, "Kate Russell's father gets to see her only one afternoon a week. I'm sure he'd rather have her to himself during that time."

Before proceeding with the business at hand, George asked Bill Taylor if he had ever seen the Peabody ducks.

"Oh, yes," Bill said.

"It's strange," George said. "I've passed through the lobby on several occasions, but I guess I never looked."

"Maybe the ducks hadn't come down yet. Or maybe they'd gone back up. The sight to see is at 10 o'clock in the morning. They march from the elevator to the fountain in the center where they spend the day. Quite the event—fanfare, drumroll, and all."

"Back to Mrs. Bellcraft—has anyone paid a visit since she broke her leg?"

"Yours truly. Twice."

"Good. How's the old girl doing?"

"You'll be interested to know," Bill said, "that she is mentioning Memorial Presbyterian in her will. A healthy sum, I suspect."

George thought of the amount that was coming to him personally from his father's estate. It would hardly be judged a healthy amount by the standards of Memorial

Presbyterian, but, thanks be to God, it was healthy enough to cover Robert Ashton's "token" fees.

❦ ❦ ❦

The regular monthly meeting of the session of Memorial Presbyterian Church was getting under way. The coffee drinkers had their foam cups full of the less-than-good brew that was available from the machine outside the door. The cold-drink drinkers opened their cans and were ready. Those who indulged in neither coffee nor cold drinks appeared markedly serious by comparison.

Harry Beckham was not indulging.

George was swilling a Diet Pepsi.

George could sense that something was up even before Harry Beckham got the floor.

"Pastor," Harry said when he did get the floor, "this is going to be difficult."

George realized that his premonition was right. He waited.

"We the elders of Memorial Presbyterian Church find it our duty—"

Sweet Martha's solo, George thought. He should have known it would hit the fan somewhere.

It was not Sweet Martha's solo. Though it might have played a part, that was not the whole thing.

Yesterday's sermon, he was told, was, if not heresy, dangerously close to it.

"The God we worship in this church is the sovereign God," Harry said, "and there is no risk in him. The God we worship is the God who called Abram out of the land of Ur and made of him a great nation. There was no risk in his following God, the risk would have been in his not doing so. The God we worship in this church is the God who called the young David to slay Goliath. The young David took no risk, for the Lord our God was with him. The God we worship in this church is the God who called out to Peter to walk upon the water. There was no risk when Peter stepped out of the boat. There was no risk until Peter took his eyes off the Lord and looked down at the waves. Need I go on? I see, Pastor, that you wish to comment. Please do."

"From a human standpoint," George said, "there was risk. From God's viewpoint, of course, there was not. But we are human and we must express ourselves in the language that we understand."

"You spoke of taking *chances* with Christ. Such language is unacceptable."

"Chances *in* Christ."

"You see a difference?"

"Yes, I do," George said.

Harry smiled condescendingly and shook his head as if dumbfounded. He said, "Well, Pastor, it's the opinion of this session that you have taken too many chances yourself recently. I speak not only of your choice of vocabulary. It has come to our attention that you took communion to the man who murdered Mrs. Templeton. A highly questionable move in itself, but especially since you went alone, knowing that our rule allows private communion only when an elder accompanies the pastor. You did know of that rule, did you not?"

"Yes. But the situation was extreme in my mind. I confess that I did break that rule when I communed the man charged with the murder of Mrs. Templeton." George secretly mustered a sense of humor, realizing that Harry Beckham would have been all the more accusing had he known that real wine was used.

"We understand that this took place after you received the blow on your head, which would mitigate things to some degree. But I have in my pocket a copy of a letter from a woman in Florence, Alabama. It describes an incident that took place *before* that unfortunate happening. Would you like for me to read the letter or shall we stop here?"

George knew there was no way that Harry Beckham or the other elders would understand his explanation of what that woman had seen through the window.

He said, "Are you asking for my resignation?"

The power elder executed a slight bow, as if to thank George for making it easy. "That would be the ideal solution," he said. He went on to state that they were offering him nine months' salary as separation pay, the nine-month period having been arrived at by giving him a year and then subtracting the three months of his recent leave.

He and his family could continue to occupy the house, the manse owned by the church, for a reasonable length of time.

George said nothing.

Harry Beckham reminded him that he could request a hearing at Presbytery if he wished to plead his case.

"I do not wish to plead anything," George said, barely above a whisper. "And now I may be excused?" He rose from his chair and left the room.

❦ ❦ ❦

He turned the television off when he got home and Margaret told him that he was rude, she had been watching. Then she looked at him and her expression changed and she asked what was the matter.

This was the hard part—telling it. George almost felt that it might not be true if he didn't put it into spoken words.

"Where is Lindley?" he asked.

"Taking a bath."

"Good. I don't want her to know the news quite yet."

"What news?"

"The church has given me my walking papers."

"You mean they've let you go?"

"They've let me go."

"You're *fired?*"

"I'm fired."

Margaret burst into tears. As George continued, his wife looked at him through a river. When he got to the business about the letter from Alabama, she protested that she had neither shown the letter nor mentioned it to anyone.

"Where is it?" he said. "I'd like to read it again. I can't remember exactly what she said."

"I don't have it."

"Oh."

"I tore it up" she told him. Then she said, "Wait a minute. What's going on here? You think I gave it to that bully, don't you? I tell you, I tore that letter into a thousand pieces."

"It could be that Alberta Wilcox sent Harry a letter of his own. She always was a busybody. Getting a letter to the right person would not have stumped her."

"But you're still wondering—yes, I can see it in your eyes—you're still wondering if I had something to do with it. You're thinking that I might have made a copy of the letter and mailed it to Harry." Margaret flew from the room and through the door to the carport and out into the yard.

George was following her. "Sweetheart," he said, "sweetheart—it's all right, it's all right. What you see in my eyes is pain, but not that pain."

He caught up with her and pulled her into his arms.

It seemed that she couldn't let the subject die. "After all," she said, "why would I want you destroyed?"

They stood there in the yard holding each other. In the summer night above them a jetliner kicked back its engines in preparation for descent. They were still standing there in the same embrace when, minutes later, a jetliner, still lifting, passed over them on its eastward flight.

"Where will we go?" Margaret asked.

"I love you, Margaret," George breathed into her ear.

"Where will we live? What will we do? What will we eat?" The womanly questions came slowly, from deep inside her.

On the tip of his tongue was a perfectly good Scripture verse. *Trust in the Lord with all your heart and lean not on your own understanding. In all your ways acknowledge him and he will direct your paths.*

He chose not to quote it at the moment.

He said again, "I love you, Margaret." He wanted that to suffice for now.

"Where do you plan to apply?"

"Hey, I haven't had time to think about it yet."

"It's scary."

"Not really scary."

"Really scary," Margaret said.

"Well—sort of."

"Will this mark go against you wherever you go?"

"All I can tell you right now is that the cloud has lifted from this place."

George briefly recounted the history of the tabernacle in the Old Testament, how God led his people by a cloud that hovered over the tabernacle. How they camped wherever the cloud stopped. How they packed up and left whenever the cloud moved on.

"I wish I had your faith," she said.

"That's funny," he said. "On many occasions I've wished that I had yours."

"What about —what are their names?—that couple?"

"Who? Oh. Carl and Dee."

"What about them?"

"I'll make it a point to keep in touch. I'll have to. Not only because they're my responsibilty, legally, but because—"

"Because of Christ," Margaret said.

"Because of Christ."

They turned and walked toward the house. The gardenia bush that Margaret had planted beside the carport was beginning to bloom. High above, beneath the stars that were telling each other the story of creation, another jet was climbing.

"Let's get practical," Margaret said. "What do you plan to do, say, tomorrow?"

"First off, we're taking Lindley down to see the Peabody ducks."

The poet, in her bathrobe, had come to the door to say goodnight.

"Have you two been out there smooching?" she said.

If you liked this book,
check out these great titles from
Lion Publishing . . .

In the gentle tradition of James Herriott and Miss Read, Jan Karon tells the heartwarming story of an Episcopal priest and the wonderfully unique people he serves in the village of Mitford, North Carolina. Seen through the eyes of Father Tim, the village becomes a kind of extended family—loving and lovable, yet bursting with secrets, heartaches, hopes, fears, failures, and surprises. Told with abounding wit and charm, the story of Father Tim is one that fiction readers will treasure for years to come.

At Home in Mitford
by Jan Karon
ISBN: 0-74592-629-0

In the small village of Sandford, everyone gets into the act when a TV crew comes to film a broadcast for Palm Sunday. You'll meet producer Jan Harding and her hardworking, enthusiastic crew. You'll also come to know local people of all ages and talents who are drawn into the television production including Clive Linton, the hopelessly absentminded vicar, his wife Helen, highly organized and increasingly distressed, Jack Diggens, who finds faith and purpose as he's drawn into the production, and many others. This fast-moving, wide-ranging story will make you laugh and cry, as well as give fascinating insight into the making of a television documentary.

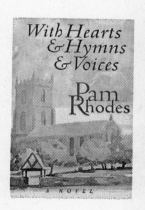

With Hearts and Hymns and Voices
by Pam Rhodes
ISBN: 0-74593-854-X